THE LEVINE PROJECT

FIGHTING BACK AGAINST A CAMPAIGN OF TERROR

DAN BALDWIN, MYLES AND KAREN LEVINE

Order this book online at www.trafford.com
or email orders@trafford.com

Most Trafford titles are also available at major online book retailers.

Print information available on the last page.

ISBN: 978-1-4907-8375-8 (sc)
ISBN: 978-1-4907-8377-2 (hc)
ISBN: 978-1-4907-8376-5 (e)

Library of Congress Control Number: 2017911704

Trafford rev. 08/22/2017

www.trafford.com
North America & international
toll-free: 1 888 232 4444 (USA & Canada)
fax: 812 355 4082

CONTENTS

"Courage is rightly esteemed the first of human qualities because, as has been said, it is the quality which guarantees all others.

Winston Churchill

"In peace there's nothing so becomes a man
As modest stillness and humility:
But when the blast of war blows in our ears,
Then imitate the action of the tiger...."

Shakespeare/Henry the Fifth

Dedication

To my mom, Delores, a lifesaver. And to my beloved dog and faithful companion, Roja, who was with us throughout the entire experience.

Karen Levine

Acknowledgements

Malena Acosta and Sterling Struckmeyer, state prosecutors who never gave up on us or our case.

FBI Special Agent Brian Nowak who was so dedicated to bringing the perpetrator to justice.

"HE DID IT AGAIN!"

Karen Levine slipped away from her comfortable bed and restful sleep and stepped into a nightmare of shock and terror, a mad scramble for life and into nearly a decade of anger, fear and frustration. Her husband, Myles (Mick) was sound asleep and their dog, Roja, was quiet. Everything seemed normal in the house, but something felt wrong. The August 2, 2009 night was a peaceful Sunday morning. The weather was hot, which is common for a Tucson summer, but the air conditioning should have kept the temperature at a comfortable level. Something was definitely wrong. Karen thought the house felt unusually warm. A broken air conditioning system combined with an Arizona summer is a guaranteed recipe for a bad day. At that moment Karen had no idea just how bad a day could become. Her next few steps would take her into years of shocking events that would change her personality, come dangerously close to ruining her husband's health, and forever alter their outlook on life.

Karen walked in the half-life between sleep and awareness to the thermostat located next to the front door. While adjusting the unit she rubbed her eyes, blinked a couple of times and glanced out to the front yard. A nerve-shattering ugliness assaulted her as she stared unbelieving at the horrible mess that a few hours earlier had been a pleasant, well-tended yard. Shock and disbelief turned quickly to full realization. She clutched her fists and fought back a powerful urge to pound the wall.

"He did it again!" she screamed.

The front of their house was scarred with frightening messages - apparently Mexican gang graffiti. And swastikas, there were lots of those, too. The yard was an ugly, stinking mess coated in oil, dead animals, and packing peanuts. The smell of human feces was unmistakable. She had been through this before – back in 2008.

Karen screamed at the top of her voice, "Mick! He did it again!"

She scrambled to the bedroom, awoke Mick and the two hurried to the front door to get a better look at the damage. The door was sealed shut from the outside. Later they would learn that an industrial grade sealant had been used to trap them inside. They attempted to open windows, but they were also sealed. He and Karen called 911 as they sought escape by moving through the house into the attached garage. The automatic garage door was sealed shut, too. In pain and fearful of what might happen next, they kept talking to the 911 operator as they hurried as fast as possible to the back door. It was not sealed, but outside they faced another nightmare. Someone had placed a bucket in their pathway and a foul-smelling substance was burning in that bucket. It sizzled and sent sparks and a plume of foul-smelling smoke into the air – chlorine gas! The gas created what became a dangerous cloud that eventually forced the evacuation of the entire neighborhood.

The 911 operator said neighbors had been making complaints about strangers in the area, clouds of smoke, and a foul odor. The police were already on the scene. Mick and Karen saw the cops on a road behind their back yard. As the couple made their way across their back yard Karen wondered, "What the hell is next? My house burns down? A bomb goes off? Is he out there with a rifle?"

Once more Todd Russell Fries entered, violently, the lives of Karen and Mick Levine.

Mick, once he and his wife were a safe distance from the danger, looked back to his house and shook his head. "That son of a bitch. "He did it again!"

CHAPTER ONE

WARMING UP TO ARIZONA

Mick Levine is an upbeat, friendly and pleasantly aggressive guy who enjoys an active and aggressive lifestyle. He is as outspoken as he is outgoing. You always know where you stand with Mick. Karen is much the same way. She is open, friendly, bright, but not shy about expressing her feelings. They had a good life in Illinois, a life full of friends and family, good times, and great memories. And cold weather. Bitterly cold temperatures didn't just hover below zero, they took up residence. As the temperature dropped each year their misery index rose with equal speed.

Each year the summers seemed to be shorter and shorter, but the winters more bitter and biting. Each season the wind cut closer to the bone. The ice and snow and the days of forced entrapment in one's own home by inclement weather were wearing them down. To make matters worse, each year took a great toll on Mick's health. His body wasn't living up to his desire to be out and about. He is an insulin dependent diabetic and has been since he was a kid.

He's had multiple heart attacks and open heart surgery, which came close to doing more harm than good. He says, "The old term that whatever can go wrong will go wrong definitely applied to that surgery. They fixed my heart, but because I'm a diabetic they botched the surgery." The clamp that holds a patient's ribs apart during the surgery damaged his intercostal nerves. The damage meant Mick suffered serious pain 365 days a year 24 hours a day. Serious fatigue was a constant problem. "I couldn't work. I was in a lot of pain. I couldn't go outside. I couldn't do a lot of walking. I couldn't do anything. Looking out to another cold and windy day, I thought, 'We just don't need to be here anymore.'"

Here was Chicago, home to the infamous Chicago winter, blow-you-over winds, snow and ice covered everything. The cold and the humidity that bored the cold right into a man's bones was getting to be a burden on Mick, a burden that every year became increasingly painful. Karen and Mick decided it was time to head south to find a warmer climate. "I was retired in Chicago. I was ill. I couldn't handle the weather anymore. We had to do something if we were ever going to stop all this suffering," Mick says.

The deciding moment arrived while on vacation in Mexico. Mick suffered another heart attack. "That brought a lot of things into focus," Karen says. Mick says, "The thought of going back to more of those Chicago winters was just too much." The "what next" question was constantly on their minds.

The answer appeared to be Florida. "The Sunshine State" seemed ideal. Even the nickname radiated a warm welcome. The climate was stable year round and the state offered a wealth of retirement communities. Florida is a diverse state with a large population of retirees from the northern states and a lot of winter guests or "snowbirds" as they are called. "Let's take a road trip and check it out," Karen says.

Mick was up for the trip, even an extended road trip. Provided they took things easy he would have no trouble or serious health issues along the way. Mick was excited about the prospect of moving to the Gulf Coast. He had lived near water all his life. He enjoyed being on the water, water sports and just the scenic beauty of rivers, lakes and oceans. Florida's sunny shores held out the promise of all this and more. They scheduled a trip that included a stop in Boulder, CO to see his brother and then a drive down to Arizona to see his ex-sister-in-law in Scottsdale and another brother in Tucson. The next step was to head east through New Orleans and then to check out various possible homes and communities in Florida. Each mile would bring them closer to a warmer environment and, at some point along the way, a better and more carefree life.

The trip was tiring, but a lot of fun. And it came to a surprising end in Tucson. Mick and Karen like to move things along at a fast pace. When something should be done they believe it should be done right and right away. That philosophy extends to major decisions in their lives. Karen says, "When we finally got to Tucson, and we stayed here for quite some time, and we loved it here. We loved the weather and we decided not to go to Florida. We decided to change all our plans and move here. That was it. We love it. Let's find a place. This is home."

Good fortune seemed to smile on the couple. Mick's brother was in real estate and he was delighted to show the Chicago transplants his community. One of the places he took them was Dove Mountain development in Heritage Highlands, a gated, age-restricted, golf community in the Tortolita Mountains just northwest of Tucson in the community of Marana. Dove Mountain was located in the Chihuahuan Desert of southern Arizona which offers spectacular scenery and incredible views. The fast moving yellows, oranges and reds of sundown have inspired artists for generations. Additionally, the area they were most interested in backed up to the 2400 acre Tortolita Preserve, which guaranteed that they would continue to enjoy those spectacular desert views. In less than two months they were the community's newest residents.

They experienced immediately more benefits than just great views. Since before the days of tubercular Doc Holiday men and women have moved out West to better their health. Mick soon found out why. He says, "I felt good here. I thought, 'This is where I want to be.'" His brother pointed out that one of the reasons Mick felt so much better is due to Tucson's lack of humidity, especially compared to a Deep South coastal state like Florida. They headed back to Chicago to prepare for the big move. Finally, the excited couple finished packing, made all the necessary arrangement and waved a goodbye to Chicago. A new life, a better and more carefree way of living awaited in Arizona.

Before heading back to the "Windy City" they may have seen a television commercial featuring Todd Russell Fries, a portly man sitting in a helicopter promoting a company known as Burns Power Washing. If they did, the images and messages perhaps found their way into the corners of memory. In a surprisingly short period of time the couple from Chicago and the pilot from the desert would face each other in business, in court, and in a life-or-death nightmare in a dark Tucson night.

Dove Mountain is an upscale retirement community in Marana, an upscale community over-looking Tucson. Features important to seniors include, an 18-hole golf course, tennis courts, clubhouse, and proximity to dining, entertainment, shopping, scenic parks and other offerings of the nearby city. Mick and Karen appeared to be moving into an ideal life. They immediately fell in love with the community and the desert environment. Even though neither cared much for playing golf, the course added to the beauty of their new home and the value of their property. Their neighbors were open and friendly, too. Karen says, "It was 'instant people' around. We knew we wouldn't be lonely when we first arrived because you could just go to the clubhouse and meet people and make friends. It wasn't like a neighborhood where you just have neighbors, but nobody comes out. Most of the people were friendly to new arrivals as soon as they showed up."

Mick says, "We were living the good life the minute we moved in. It was a relaxed life. It was quiet. And down here my health was better because I wasn't in humidity. I was still in pain, but I did better here." They spoke to neighbors and his brother and did some research on their own and soon found a good nephrologist to keep an eye on Mick's kidney condition and an internist to monitor his diabetes. "I was doing okay," he says.

They made friends and even joined a Corvette Club. Mick owned a white, automatic 1986 Corvette with an original cloth interior – one of only a small number of those models built. For an automobile fan or collector or even someone who just likes to see the lines of a beautiful automobile it was a treasure. Mick took justifiable pride in his car and he took equal pride in keeping it in immaculate shape. The club was another place to make friends, get to know the community and to settle in to their new home in the company of other people with many similar interests.

Life was good. The newcomers were active and trying new things and becoming members of a community. The shift in climate, culture and quality of life was enormous and they welcomed the changes.

Karen was even able to transfer her work from the Windy City to the Old Pueblo (Tucson). Karen is an expert at barter. Many people today think the bartering trade as a thing of the past. Some believe it went the way of the old tinker riding a mule and selling his wares from village to village back in the good old days before the horseless carriage. Nothing could be further from the truth. Bartering is an active element of 21st Century business and industry. She would sign up business owners who would get credit for the value of their services with another business owner. The process is similar to banking except that the account uses credit instead of cash. She says, "I wanted to stay with what I did in Chicago. I knew the work and I was good at it. My boss at the time knew of my reputation from Chicago and he hired me to handle bartering for the firm. I decided to just work here instead of having to work out of two cities. My boss at that time said, 'I'm going to give you some credit you can use for things you need to get started in your new home.' We needed things for the house. He gave me a salary and bonuses, too. I was doing very well."

The transition had been easy and they were enjoying an entirely new lifestyle in an entirely new and exciting environment.

"We were having fun," Karen says.

"No doubt about it," Mick says.

Other than Mick's ongoing health issues and the natural readjustments to a new community, the challenges they faced were pretty typical for a home owner. They noticed only one small problem. The house and yard was in good shape, but the driveway needed a little bit of minor work. It was streaked with unsightly black tire marks.

The streets in Dove Mountain are asphalt which is easily picked up on automobile tire treads and just as easily transferred to the neighborhood driveways. Most homes in the development have paint-covered driveways to help obscure the inevitable dark streaks. Karen was tired of seeing the dark streaks on their long, curved driveway. She decided to have theirs painted. She found a business owner who put in pebble tec pool and spa surfaces. These surfaces resemble natural backgrounds such as beaches or riverbeds and help disguise the unsightly asphalt streaks. The company also used the same technology to surface sidewalks and driveways. A pebble tec surface appealed to Karen's design sense and also to her practical, safety-conscience mind. A textured surface would be safer for walking in Arizona's summer monsoons which can bring powerful rain storms. Ice and frost in the lower elevations around Tucson are rare, but they do show up some winters and can make walking on pavement an adventure. Resurfacing and then painting the driveway would solve the practical as well as the aesthetical challenges.

"I really wanted something different, something with real style." The company's representative came up with something that seemed to fit her needs.

"She didn't want the same thing as everyone else, so he came up with something different. The textures were different. The colors were different. We wouldn't stick out like a sore thumb, but what she picked out wouldn't be a cookie-cutter imitation of every other home in the neighborhood. This was our home and we wanted to make it *distinctly* our home," Mick says.

They had him do the driveway, sidewalk, and patio and everything looked nice for a while. Despite the ingrained, textured surface of the driveway, tire marks soon began showing. Cleaning them off proved to be "a disaster." Nothing Karen could do would remove the dark streaks. Karen called the businessman back to get him to honor his commitment, but he had moved to Utah. When she tracked him down, he said, "Honey, I'm not in Tucson anymore." Mick and Karen could either live with the mess that the contractor had created or they could find a company managed by someone who could undo the damage and then do the job the way it was supposed to be done.

"That's when I found Burns Power Washing," Karen says. Perhaps it was a faint memory of seeing that commercial with the chubby man in the helicopter that prodded her to make that call. Perhaps it was just the ill-luck of the draw. Karen called and spoke to Todd Russel Fries.

And that's when they found real trouble.

CHAPTER TWO

GETTING BURNED

K aren almost gave up finding the answer to cleaning and keeping clean the driveway. She consulted with a number of contractors, but each one turned down the work. Essentially, they said, to do what was necessary to achieve the look, reliability and safety margins required, a contractor would have to practically rebuild the driveway from the dirt up. Because of the significant amount of time, equipment and manpower involved, the job was just too challenging to be worth the effort for either party. Karen does not discourage easily, so she kept looking, making calls and asking questions. One evening a television commercial for Burns Power Washing caught her attention. The owner was his own spokesman and he talked confidently about his company and what he and his crew was able to do. He offered a wide range of services and he was a local businessman. "I thought it odd that Fries used his helicopter in his commercials, but I guess that made him stand out from all the rest. It must have worked for him because it got our attention," Mick says.

Karen called and made an appointment for the owner, Todd Russell Fries, to come out, examine the property, and give them an estimate. *It's just an estimate. What could we lose?* She thought. Years later Mick and Karen Levine would be amazed at how much a simple phone call could cost in not only terms of time and money, but in heartache, worry, frustration and fear.

7

Burns Power Washing operated out of a strip mall office in north Tucson. The business, like its owner, was low-key, but it appeared to be a stable and successful member of the business community. The company's promotional material promised professional service from courteous uniformed employees who used modern equipment. Services were guaranteed and the company was licensed, bonded and a member of the Power Washers of North America. Fries presented a professional appearance in his ads, helicopter and all, so what could go wrong?

Fries was a portly and not too tall man in his early forties who had a soft voice. He had buzz-cut black hair and was balding in the back. A thin moustache and baggy eyes accentuated his round face. In dress, appearance and attitude he seemed like an average small-business owner. Like most Arizona residents he was not a native of the state. He was born in Syracuse, NY and moved to The Copper State as a child. He graduated from high school and attended community college before serving four years in the Marine Corp. He returned to Tucson, married and is the father of two adult children. He and his wife divorced in the nineties. Although he did not drink alcohol or use illegal drugs, he took medication for high blood pressure. He was, to all appearances, a pretty normal guy.

"We should have remembered that old saying – appearances can be deceiving," Karen says.

His presentation was polite and professional, and confident. His business seemed well-established and reliable. Burns Power Washing had a number of significant contracts, including doing work for the University of Arizona, Davis-Monthan Air Force Base, area hospitals, businesses and residences. He had trucks, equipment, chemicals and from four to ten employees depending on the amount of work being done.

Fries spoke with authority and seemed to know his business. He appeared to be someone they could trust and who would be easy to work with. After examining the property he spoke confidently of his company's ability to solve her problem. They could fix the driveway and would blend it with the sidewalk so that they wouldn't have to apply a coating. The texture would be different, but the look would be the same and she and Mick would save some money on the project. He promised to get the color right and do a thoroughly professional job in a short period of time.

According to Mick, Fries said, "This won't take long, about a day or two and we'll wrap it up. It's going to be fine. It's not going to be a problem." He spoke with such easy confidence that Mick and Karen forgot about the reluctance of other contractors to take on the job. Fries and Karen agreed on a price, terms and a timetable. The total job would cost $2500. The deal was made and Karen paid him half upfront in cash with the other half due upon completion.

Karen did not see any "red flags" during their negotiations although Fries seemed a bit full of himself. "I thought he was very cocky and that he believed he 'knew everything' like a Mr. Know-It-All, and that there was nothing he could not do. So, it wouldn't be a disaster like the other contractors had indicated. He acted very professional. I wasn't analyzing his behavior, I mean his personality. I just wanted him to do the job right and if that meant putting up with his ego for a short while, so be it."

The Burns Power Washing truck pulled up two days later. Fries was with them, but he only stayed long enough to tell the crew what to do. He left the jobsite quickly saying that the Levines and their property were in good hands. His eight man crew unloaded their equipment and began their tasks. They worked hard and seemed attentive to the job at hand, but Mick immediately noticed a problem with their methodology, recognizing the likely unsuccessful outcome of their efforts. Prior to putting in a new surface the old textured surface had to be ground down and roughed up. That type of work requires industrial grade grinding equipment. The tool the Burns crew was using to grind down the surface of the concrete wasn't remotely suitable for concrete work. It was a floor buffer – the kind janitors and service personnel use in office buildings to polish floors. Mick says, "I was watching this stuff because I was coming and going running errands around the house. The idea Fries had was to rough up what was on the surface and paint over it. That's good. The problem his crew was having was basic – they had the wrong tool for the job. They couldn't do what they had been brought there to do. A crew ten times their size with ten times the same equipment couldn't have accomplished anything more. Nothing would rough up. The men worked an entire day basically trying to shine up concrete. The job was supposed to take just a couple of days, but by the time they went home they had accomplished nothing. This did not give me a good feeling."

That feeling returned the next day with the return of the Burns crew. They still tried to remove the surface of the concrete with floor buffers. Floor buffer pads are commonly made of natural fibers such as wool or from foam rubber. Neither will have much effect on concrete other than to kick up a little dust. Things didn't work out for the crew any easier the second time at bat. Mick wondered if the men were just going through the motions because that's what the boss told them to do or if they really didn't understand the mechanics relating to the application of rotating foam rubber to rock-hard cement. He finally joined them and said, "You guys know you're wasting your time. The only way you're going to get this done is by getting on your knees and grinding off what's on the cement with the right kind of equipment. You need something that's actually going to grind it down."

Surely this process was not what Fries had planned for a quick, down-and-dirty job with a fast payoff. The job required more specialized equipment, more time on the job for his crew, and an entirely different approach. All of this would have to come out of his dwindling if not already non-existent profit margin.

"He was trying to do the cheapest possible job. I understand that, but that really wasn't our problem. He knew the job going in, or with his experience he should have known better," Karen says.

Karen says, "All we wanted was for him to deliver what he had promised – no more no less."

Fries had already invested a full crew and two days of work with no progress. The only real grinding down was on the buffers his men used. His costs were mounting and his customers were seeing no results. The eight men returned another day and began working on the concrete surface with hand-held grinders suited for the job. After a couple of weeks of working on their knees the crew finally ground away the surface.

A job Fries had hoped would be completed within a couple of days had so far taken nearly three weeks. He was not a happy man. A down-and-dirty, quick job for quick money had turned into a money pit. He had grossly underestimated what the job would require. Karen says that to his credit he never asked them for more money. At that time he realized he had created his own problem and he seemed to be committed to honoring his agreement. "He showed nothing of the craziness that would hit us later. From the way he acted we never expected what happened later," Karen says. The grinding was at last completed and it was time to paint the driveway. The home owners association had to approve of any painting work, so Mick and Karen selected a green that matched the color of their house. The driveway was finally painted, but they had to wait eight days before using it to allow time for the paint to set and dry. "We thought that was the end of it. We didn't ever think that it was the beginning of something so horrible," Karen says.

Mick was first to notice a problem with the work. Despite the paint, anyone could plainly see grinding marks on the surface. The driveway looked far worse than before the work had begun. Karen's response was half-sad and half-angry. "They've ruined my driveway. I mean, we paid good money just to ruin our own home." They soon discovered another problem. After all that time, extra costs, and work Burns Power Washing hadn't solved their original problem. The streets in Dove Mountain are asphalt which adheres to automobile tires, especially in Arizona's hot summers. Like paint absorbed and then applied by rollers, that dark and sticky substance gets deposited on concrete driveways, forming thick, black stains – tire marks. The driveway was still getting stained with asphalt from the street. Every day added a new layer of black streaks and embedded the existing marks deeper into the driveway.

The deal they had agreed on was to have the driveway painted in such a way that the stains could be washed away with a stream from a garden hose. Hosing down the driveway not only failed to remove the stains, it revealed an even more serious problems and one that created a legitimate health hazard. The surface became slippery when wet and caused Karen to slip and fall practically every time she attempted to clean the driveway. Karen is very close to her mother who is a frequent guest at their home. The slippery nature of the driveway presented a serious health hazard not only to the elderly woman, but to anyone stepping on the surface. A potentially hazardous event occurred one rainy day when their mailman slipped and took a bad fall. Fortunately, he wasn't harmed. "Beyond worrying about hurting someone, we realized we could be open to a lawsuit if someone fell and got hurt," Karen says.

She called Fries and apprised him of the situation and of their serious concerns. He said, "Well, we have 325-350 days of the year here when it's sunny. But, when it does rain try not to wear any high heels or go on the driveway. But it doesn't rain here much, so you'll be fine." His lack of concern for his client, her neighbors and his own reputation didn't seem to be a factor now that he thought the job was done. Karen says, "He told me my main concerns were cleaning the driveway so he wanted to make it easy to clean the driveway. I mean, come on. I couldn't even stand on the driveway when it was wet. You shouldn't have to tell a contractor, 'Oh, and be sure to make sure it's safe and doesn't kill anyone.'"

Apparently Fries was counting on the newcomer's lack of knowledge about their new home state when he made those "it's all going to be just fine" statements. Arizona is known for its bright and sunny skies, but the state doesn't enjoy 325 – 350 rain-free days a year. Arizonans know and prepare for the annual summer monsoon season, which brings enormous dust clouds and thunderstorms that drench the desert. The state is studded with street and highway signs reading Do Not Enter When Flooded because those sudden and powerful rains can turn a dry wash, ravine or low places in the road into dangerous and sometimes deadly traps. Streets and driveways aren't spared. Mick says, "We had just moved here, so we didn't know about the monsoon, but that was his excuse. Then we found out that to do this process on a surface like our driveway you have to use silicon in the top layer of paint, which won't let you slip. It's clear, of course, and it's in the paint so you don't see it, but it grips so you don't slip when it's wet. There was no silicon used on our driveway. He just used a shiny, glossy paint." The new surface had turned a residential driveway into a potential slip 'n slide, one of those kids playthings from Wham-O.

"That's' just what could have happened to anyone stepping on our drive way in the rain. Wham! And then Oh!" Mick says.

Because Fries had skimped on the budget the driveway also developed unsightly blotches easily visible to the neighbors and anyone driving by. The HOA called to complain. Their driveway had become a stain on the neighborhood in the opinion of the HOA members. The paint job was faulty and did not match the color of the house. Instead of the specified green, it had been coated in an unattractive yellow-green that clashed with the residence. Every aspect of the job had been botched, badly botched.

When contacted about the problems Fries gave Karen a hard time. She had no way of knowing at the time, but Fries had something of a questionable past in dealing with others. He had been charged but not convicted of four misdemeanor s dating back to 1996: two charges for shoplifting, one for assault and another for disorderly conduct. She wouldn't let go and insisted that he and his company live up to their agreement. "It wasn't our fault that he used the wrong materials. It wasn't our fault that he lost money. But it was definitely his fault that the job was a mess." Fries finally agreed, but said he would have to charge an extra $500 and the Levines would have to be responsible for providing the paint. That seemed, at the time, to be the most reasonable approach. At least, they would finally get an attractive and safe driveway. Fries specified the type of silicon-paint they should get. They purchased the designated amount from a local Sherman-Williams dealer and directly from a manager also specified by Fries. They paid upfront so that the Burns crew could pick it up and go straight to the jobsite. "We were ready to wrap this thing up and get Todd Fries and his company out of our lives," Mick says.

The crew from Burns came back and repainted the driveway. Fries told them to stay off the driveway for a while to let it set and dry. The job, at last, appeared to have been done right. After a few weeks of use Karen went out with her garden hose to wash down the driveway. She stepped on the wet driveway, slipped and fell. Mick and Karen are not in the construction trades. Like most people hiring out residential work they depend on the expertise of the firms and the people they do business with. They called the manager from Sherwin Williams to take a look at the botched project. He said that the paint used didn't have enough sand – enough silicon. In another effort to skimp on the budget Fries had specified a lower cost paint – the wrong paint for the needs of the job.

Karen called Fries for the third time. She told him she and Mick were very unhappy customers. The job wasn't done right. The driveway was still a mess. The HOA was on their backs. They were vulnerable to a lawsuit if someone fell and got hurt. He had to make this thing right and he needed to do it right away.

His response was so-so. "He really wasn't that mad. He knew what he did. He knew he did it wrong," Karen says. Mick says that Fries didn't put up much of an argument even though it was obvious he was not happy about the situation. The Burns crew returned, roughed up the surface and repainted the driveway. Again, Fries told them to let it set and dry before walking on it. They half joked that they should purchase "Danger. Do Not Enter" signs around their driveway. All joking stopped when Fries said he needed another $400.

Now, Mick was not a happy man. "We didn't pay for the silicon because supposedly we had already paid for what he wanted. But he insisted I had to pay him another $400 for his labor. He paid for the paint and silicon that time, but I already paid for it. I wasn't going to pay for it again."

They agreed on a 50/50 payment plan. Mick and Karen would pay $200 up front and $200 when the job was completed to their satisfaction. Fries added an unusual stipulation. He said they were not to make out the check to Burns Power Washing. He wanted them to make it to him personally. Mick and Karen agreed. They really didn't care which entity got the money provided the money was applied to the job and that the job would be done correctly as promised. They looked forward to putting the entire matter behind them.

That was not to be the case.

A big "wham!" and a painful and frightening "oh!" would soon follow.

CHAPTER THREE

"KAREN, SOMETHING HAPPENED TO YOUR HOUSE!"

Mick is on disability. With his medication and visits to physicians the family cash flow can get tight. As with most families, money management is important, especially after making a major life change and adjusting to a new lifestyle in a new environment. Mick and Karen lived comfortably, but not so comfortably that they felt like "eating" several hundred dollars. They are sound financially because they keep a tight rein on income and outgo. The first time they had worked with Burns Power Washing, Mick and Karen paid Fries $500 in two post-dated checks made out to Burns Power Washing Company. They got an inkling of Fries' money management skills when he cashed the second check first. Mick was also concerned that a bank would cash a post-dated check. That double whammy of financial mismanagement caused four other Levine checks to bounce, an embarrassing situation and one that could have affected their credit rating and relationships with creditors. Frustration with Fries' work ethic turned to embarrassment and anger over the man's lack of basic business skills. Mick called Fries who apologized, blamed the foul up on his bookkeeper, and said that he would cover the overdraft fees, which he did. "Okay, mistakes happen, so I figure we're dealing with someone who is a bit sloppy, but fairly legitimate. At that point we just wanted to get this job done and put the whole thing behind us," Mick says.

Still, Burns Power Washing was $1000 over the original estimate. And the job still wasn't done to their satisfaction. In fact, their driveway was now in worse condition then when they began the project.

After the Burns crew finished, the project's supervisor, David Trujillo, came to the door and said they'd completed the work. He asked for payment of $400 as agreed. Mick said, "This is what I'm going to do. You call Todd now and tell him you're getting two checks. One is for $200 and it's good right now. The other is for $200 and will be good in a month – if nobody falls. That's my stipulation on final payment."

"I was just tired of paying for work we weren't getting. He needed to know we weren't going to put up with any more foul ups," Karen says.

Trujillo called Fries, informed him of the situation, and was told to accept the checks.

"That's the end of it we thought," Mick says.

Thing were just beginning to go to hell, instead.

Trujillo later told investigators that the stop-payment on the check seriously upset Fries. According to Trujillo, Fries called Karen "a fucking bitch." As what he would come to call "the Levine Project," Fries said he wanted to get back at Karen. He wanted to execute his plan on Halloween because all the noise would disguise the activity. Note that according to his employees Fries wanted to get even with Karen – not Mick and Karen and not the Levines. Karen. And this may be a clue to the motive for Fries' otherwise unexplained reasons for his odd and dangerous actions.

A month passed and no one slipped or fell on the repaired driveway. Another month passed, again without incident. Mick noticed that Fries had not cashed the second check. He called Fries to tell him to go ahead and cash the check. Fries wasn't in, so he left a message. Again, he thought that was the end of the matter. Some time passed and the check still hadn't been cashed. Mick wanted to make sure everything was on the up and up so he called again, left more messages, but never got a response. The check remained uncashed. Mick and Karen wanted to get that check off their books, keep their finances in line, and mainly move along and put the whole thing behind them.

Mick says, "We don't want loose ends when it comes to family finances, but Fries still wouldn't call me back. I decided that the only way

I was going to get a response out of him was to stop payment on the other check, figuring that when he can't cash it he will call me back. And I'd issued him another check right away."

He called their bank, Wells Fargo, on a Friday afternoon and told them that he was missing a check. It had been out for months, he couldn't contact the person it was written to, and that he needed to stop payment. The bank complied and put a stop payment on it. The next day, Saturday they got a call from the Oro Valley branch.

Mick took the call and was told that someone showed up with the check and the bank had cashed it. The Levines have Caller ID, so they knew the call was coming from their bank. It wasn't apparently a scam, but something was clearly amiss. "I said, there's a stop payment on the check and you cashed it? That's your problem. I'm not making it good."

At that point the person at the bank changed the story. Contrary to what was said earlier, the bank had not cashed the check and had informed the man with the check of that fact. Mick was stunned by what he heard next. The banker who was cashing the check wanted to take their check and open another account with it. Mick was outside the house when he took the call. To give himself a moment to digest what he had just heard he told the person at the other end he would go inside to his office and would call back immediately.

Caller ID gave Mick the legitimate phone number of the bank, also the name of the person who said she was the head teller. He called back and asked for the head teller. The matter began to get squirrely at that point. The woman said she was only a teller, not the head teller. Mick told her that he had just spoken with her and she had identified herself as the head teller during that call. The woman said that she had never made any such call and that she didn't know what he was talking about. Mick said, "What! I just spent 15 minutes on the phone with you." Again, she insisted that she had never spoken with him. But she was just a teller and definitely not the head teller. The tone of her voice indicated that she was a bit confused by the situation, but that she was telling the truth. Apparently someone was trying to pull a fast one on Mick and Karen and at the same time the bank.

Confused himself, more than a little bit surprised, and getting just a bit frustrated, Mick asked for Mr. Jones, the branch manager – the man he had gone to and suggested they open a new account with the $200 check. She responded that, like herself, Mr. Jones was just a personal banker. He wasn't the branch manager.

This bit of information was too much. Mick told her, "Ma'am, I'm 20 minutes from your branch. I'm calling the Oro Valley police and I will have a squad meet me there. I expect you and Mr. Jones to be there when we arrive. We're going to get to the bottom of whatever is going on here."

She agreed. What else was she to do? Apparently she was as much in the dark as Mick and Karen over the matter. The police met Mick when he arrived at the bank. The teller's story was that neither of them had talked to Mick. Supposedly someone had entered the bank, sat down at Mr. Jones' desk and made the phone calls. Mr. Jones couldn't have made the call anyway because he was not even at the bank that morning. During one of the trials that followed it was determined that Fries impersonated the teller and Mr. Jones by disguising his voice with something called a Spoof Caller. It's a small electronic device that allows someone using a telephone to change a voice from male to female, female to male, or to just vary the tone of voice. The device is small, relatively inexpensive and readily available at stores and on the Internet.

The Oro Valley PD took the report. They couldn't make any sense of the event and for them that was that. Apparently no laws had been broken. No one was being harassed or threatened. No damage had been done, so the investigation was over almost as soon as it had begun. "Case closed" because to the PD there was no case to close in the first place.

The incident was, unfortunately, just the beginning of a series of challenges, harassment, threats and life-threatening actions that would drive Mick and Karen Levine from home to home and from a dream lifestyle to an ongoing nightmare – all for a small amount of money they had been trying to pay all along.

Fries called a couple of weeks later. He thanked Mick for making good on the check. Mick couldn't believe what he was hearing and said, "What are you talking about? You know damn well I stopped payment on that check. I didn't make that check good." Fries hung up. That was the last conversation Mick had with him. Mick says, "I would have told him I'd make the check good because nobody had fallen, but I didn't get the chance to do that. I felt okay you did finally make it right. I don't need the aggravation. I have enough problems in my life. It's finally right. I'll pay you your other $200, but he never contacted me again."

Fries' unusual behavior was to say the least puzzling. He was a successful businessman and successful businessmen just don't act that foolishly – especially with money on the table ready to be picked up. Unfortunately, the odd behavior didn't stop with a hang up call. It accelerated.

Representatives from other businesses were to some extent involved with the situation. For example before the power washing team came back the second time, Karen went back to the Sherwin Williams salesman to tell him about their problems with the paint. She added that she was going to contact the Better Business Bureau and file a complaint against Burns Power Washing." *His* company and *your* paint have created *our* problem and I'm very unhappy," she said.

Apparently, the salesman at Sherwin Williams notified Fries about the situation. Fries bought all his paint from this company and apparently exclusively from this salesman. Later, someone called Karen representing himself as Mr. Alverez, a manager from the BBB. Karen says, "He said he heard that I was unhappy with this company, Burns Power Washing. He told me that Burns was a very good and reputable company. The firm had an A-plus rating with the bureau. I shouldn't make a report against him. It's a great company. I should just make it right with him, straighten it out with him. He really pushed me to resolve the situation directly with Fries." She felt there was something odd, something wrong with the conversation. It just didn't seem right.

Karen wrote down the Caller ID number and called the bureau. She was told that there was no Mr. Avlerez at the bureau. They seemed as puzzled about the call as Karen. She says, "It was Todd Fries. He must have gone over to the BBB to use their phone hoping the caller ID would lend him credibility." Fries was not a member of the bureau.

Fries was brazen enough – or foolish enough – to try the same ploy twice. He called back, again attempting to disguise his voice. Karen says, "You're not any Mr. Alverez. Todd, I know this is you, so you don't have to do this impersonation." The caller stuck to his story, but Karen wasn't buying his pitch. "Fries said, 'I don't know what you're talking about.' He just flat out denied it and then he hung up. I knew that this so-called Mr. Alverez was Todd Fries. It was so weird."

Within a few months weird became outrageous. Later it would evolve into dangerous.

Karen and Mick thought the matter closed. Fries never called to pick up his check and they heard nothing more from Fries or anyone from Burns Power Washing. July and summer turned into fall and eventually Halloween. This was a traditional girl's night out for Karen. She and her mom went into town to celebrate on what was a pleasant Saturday night. Mick's kidneys were giving him some serious problems, so he stayed home.

Karen returned and went to bed. Mick, in pain, was unable to sleep, so he and their dog, Roja, sat up and watched television. Dove Mountain was a gated community, a peaceful and safe environment; Mick thought nothing about leaving the windows and doors open late at night or in the early hours of the morning. About two a.m. he closed the doors and went to bed. Roja slept on the floor nearby.

At 5:30 a.m. Nov. 1 the phone rang. Karen grabbed the phone and answered. One of their neighbors said," "I don't want you to worry, but Karen, something has happened to your house."

CHAPTER FOUR

MOVING TARGETS

A few moments earlier Karen's neighbor stepped out of his house to pick up his morning newspaper. He stretched, looked at the fading night, and breathed in the warm scents carried on a fresh desert breeze. But this morning something unpleasant, a foul odor, tainted the early morning air. The smell was strong enough to induce gagging. When he glanced up the street he saw the source of the smell. The image of the Levine's home was something out of a low-budget horror film. The whole place had been trashed. Even a quick glance in the early morning semi-darkness revealed that the work wasn't a prank by friendly high school students or kids from their car club or clubhouse. The landscaping wasn't "rolled" with toilet paper or painted with shaving cream. One glance and he knew a sick mind had been at work in his neighborhood. He rushed in and made the call to Karen.

Karen says, "The minute he said something had happened to my house I just dropped the phone and ran to the front door. I saw this horrible mess on the sidewalk – something shiny, some paint, just a real mess. I couldn't even walk out there because it covered everything." Avoiding that mess was more than a concern about ruining her house shoes. The dark and shiny gunk emitted a foul odor, perhaps from harmful chemicals. Worse still, there were dead animals and trash within it. Several carcasses had been placed near the front door. The financial damage to the property was eventually estimated to be more than

$10,000. But the cost in dollars and cents wasn't the primary concern that morning.

Karen thought to get out by going through the garage, but when she tried to open the automatic door it wouldn't lift. The motor ran as usual, but the door remained immobile.

At that point Karen couldn't take any more. Her home had been attacked and her security had been threatened. Maybe the horror wasn't over and her family was in serious danger. She screamed. "The whole neighborhood probably heard me, "she says.

Mick woke up and, forgetting his pain, rushed into the garage. He struggled with the door, but it still wouldn't open. "I couldn't get the thing to work. I hit it a couple of times. The mechanism actually broke right off the door – ripped the motor, the chain, everything." He realized they had to get outside to see just what was going on and to find out if it was still going on. "We couldn't get out the front doors because of the dead animals and the paint and everything. No way were we going to step in that junk," he says. Karen experienced a second of horror when they found the dead coyote at the front door. For a terrible second she thought the animal was Roja. "She wasn't out that night, thank God," Karen says. They scrambled through their home and escaped through the back door and were able to survey how badly their home had been trashed.

The amount of damage was shocking. Karen says, "Our neighbors couldn't believe something like that could happen in our peaceful little community. I couldn't believe it and I was right in the middle of it!" The fairy tale dream of a life of peaceful and contented retirement had turned into a very real nightmare of unbelievable proportions.

Once they had a fairly good idea of the damage they returned to the telephone, calling first the neighbors to see if they had reported the incident to the Marana Police Department. Other neighbors, early risers or people alerted by the screaming came out of their homes and were taking in the unbelievable sight. And the equally unbelievable smell. One of the neighbors volunteered that he saw somebody in the middle of the night in what he described as a weird truck, an old pickup that didn't belong in the neighborhood. It has been parked in the driveway of the vacant house directly across from Mick and Karen's home. No one living in the cul de sac owned an old pickup and none of the neighbors had overnight guests driving such a vehicle. It had to belong to the perpetrators, but unfortunately the description of the vehicle was so vague it was useless to the police. No one had seen anybody acting suspicious that morning or the evening before so there was no description of the perpetrator or perpetrators for the police to go on.

As they began to get over the initial shock and to settle down, Mick and Karen took stock of the damage that had been done to their dream home. Mick says, "The whole front of the house, driveway, sidewalk, front yard was full of paint, oil, dead animals, packing peanuts, and splattered paint all over. Blue, white, yellow paint. And it stunk. The odor was terrible." Karen says, "The shiny black goo was something called sludge oil. It smelled like dead people. It was the worst smell. Add to that the dead animals and you just can't imagine…."

Mick saw a large dead animal on the patio by the front door and for an instant he too feared that someone had killed Roja. "There was a dead animal the size of the dog right in front of the front door covered with paint and oil. We found out later it was a coyote. The first thing I did was to check the dog. Roja, thank God, was in the bedroom with Karen who was still screaming. 'My house is a mess. It stinks. Look at what they did,' she kept saying.

But as it turned out that wasn't all they did.

The sun came up and daylight revealed even more of the ugliness that had been brought to the quiet neighborhood. During one of the trials that followed, Deputy Sherifff Edward Muzala would testify that when he responded to the call he observed that the driveway was covered with motor oil and packing peanuts and that there was graffiti on the curb and garage door which included 'spray painting, male and female genitals, plus the swastikas and anarchy signs.' Muzala also noticed 'a very bad smell of dead animals and motor oil. Someone had spray painted offensive and threatening messages on the garage door.

Die Jew.
Die Jew Bitch.
Die Jew Whore.
Die Juden.

And there were swastikas. The swastikas moved the criminal acts, at least potentially, into the ugly arena of hate crimes. The investigation had not even begun at that point, so the motivation as well as the perpetrators were for the time being unknown.

Mick and Karen went to a neighbor's driveway where they sat in a golf cart and were interviewed by the Marana police who were also interviewing the neighbor who saw the suspicious truck a few hours earlier. During that conversation Mick noticed a paint-coated wallet down in the gunk coating their property. Inside was an identification card belonging to a Ms. Kaylin Hovey. The officers took it, but neither Mick nor Karen got a look at what was in it. The police were also busy taking photographs, talking to neighbors, and examining the scene.

Crime scene analysts also found a paint can that contained three latent fingerprints at the scene, one of them on the bottom of a paint can. In October, 2009 one of those fingerprints was identified as belonging to Todd Russell Fries.

Mick says, "They weren't nice at first because they're taking pictures and looking around. I'm pointing out things to them that they're not even looking at. I said, there's a big chain with a large padlock there. That doesn't belong there. None of this belongs here." There were three sets of footprints in the paint in the driveway. He also had to show them his mailbox which had been painted over. When they were about to leave, Mick insisted that they dispose of the dead coyote. "You can't leave a dead animal at my door."

After the police left, one of the neighbors came over and helped Mick clean up as much of the paint and oil as they could. There were able to clean up the sidewalk well enough so that people could walk on it without contaminating their shoes. Mick called a cleanup service and a crew arrived that day and cleaned up the oil and paint. The work was challenging. The crew had to dig up the landscaping rock, dig into the ground, take all that up and redo everything right from the ground up. The oil and paints had soaked well into the earth. The front yard looked more like an industrial waste site than a residential property.

They, and their neighbors, had to live with that foul stench for a month.

They discovered the problem with the garage door when Mick noticed an orange substance lining the edges. That substance was an industrial grade sealant which bonded the door to the driveway and to the framing around the door. Essentially, the door had been turned into a wall, which had trapped the Levines inside. They called a garage door repair company to redo the garage door. The cleanup process was time-consuming and expensive.

During the subsequent investigation the Marana Police asked if they had any conflicts that might have led to some form of retribution. There were two. One was a gardener who was the husband of a cleaning lady they had hired to trim a tree in the front yard. Instead of removing away and disposing of tree branches he threw them over the back wall into the wash. The HOA complained about the trash and the way in which the job had been handled. "So, I'm in trouble with the HOA. I didn't pay the guy. You didn't do your work I told him and that's that," Mick says.

The other conflict was with Todd Fries and Burns Power Washing.

The investigation continued and Mick and Karen continued with the struggle to clean up a seriously trashed house and a contaminated front lawn. The process of getting the place in livable condition took about a month. While this was going on Mick's health began to decline even more. The shock of the attack and the stress and effort involved with the cleanup took a terrible toll. He says, "Mentally I was totally stressed out. My diabetes was getting worse. My kidneys, already at end stage renal failure were getting worse. All because of what was going on. There was so much pressure about all this." One of the major factors in his increasing stress levels, perhaps the leading factor, was the utter confusion and lack of information about what had happened. Who could have done such a thing and why?

Karen's mother brought up and continued to bring up a significant and disturbing possibility. There was no indication that the incident was a one-time event. Things could be repeated or they could even escalate. She felt there was a very real possibility that someone was planning to commit murder. Considering the enormity of the damage, the personal nature of it and how it had been accomplished, her fears were justified.

Mick says, "Finally I said I can't stay here anymore. You're telling me someone is trying to kill us. God knows what could happen next. They pulled the gate off the wall of the compound to get in. They used the chain to pull down the facilities. If they did it once, they can do it again."

Karen could see every day the debilitating effects on her husband. The strain was also a personal challenge. She says, "We decided to move. I called the mortgage company and said I'm giving you back the house. I can't pay for all this. So I'm voluntarily giving you the house. They says, 'You can't do that.' I said I'm doing it. I'm leaving the keys in the house. It's yours. So I abandoned the house."

Todd Fries was the most likely suspect, but the evidence couldn't be tied to either the man or his business. Finally, the investigator for the Marana police told them that the investigation had hit a dead end. The department just had no more leads on the case so there was no point in continuing. Mick says, "His words to Karen were, 'Well, you can't make him (Fries) talk, so we can't prove anything.'" That was it – end of story and case closed as far as Todd Fries was concerned. The police, however, had another, wilder thought.

Karen says there was another reason for the halt. "I think the officer thought we did it to ourselves."

A grand jury was convened and Mick and Karen were accused of trashing their own home to get insurance money. Mick couldn't believe what he was hearing. "I told the officer from Marana Police, 'You think we did this to get the money that I used up to get the house fixed up from all the damage? So, what money did I plan to get from the insurance company?'"

The Marana grand jury agreed with Mick's argument. They realized that trashing your own home just to get enough money to repair the damage to the home you just trashed just didn't make sense. No indictment was handed down. They didn't hear about the grand jury until later when one of the department heads told them. "The officer was schedule to become a patrol sergeant, so he just wanted to clear his cases. I think that was his motivation," Mick says.

Unfortunately, the struggle and strain was not over. As the saying goes, "You can run, but you can't hide." It's virtually impossible to disappear today. Karen and Mick were on the move. But someone was still on their trail.

CHAPTER FIVE

INSIDE THE PRESSURE COOKER

Mick's health deteriorated rapidly in the weeks after the attack. His nephrologist warned that dialysis was becoming a very real and perhaps imminent concern. He wasn't sure just how long he could delay the procedure without greater risk to Mick's health. Mentally, the event and the uncertainty of what was happening to them and what might happen in the future took a serious toll. He says "I was even more ill than ever and it was all because of this stress. I was doing what my doctor was telling me - watching my diet, exercising and all that. I didn't want to go on dialysis. This whole thing was just eating me up. I couldn't handle it. This was all due to the incidents because I was fine until then. I can say for sure, in more ways than one Todd Fries is a health risk."

Although her health wasn't affected to the same degree, Karen suffered from the stress, too. More than being stalked, it seemed as though she and her husband were being hunted. "What had happened to us was bad enough. But, we didn't know what was next. Was this the end of it? Would it happen again? Could it get even worse? We didn't know and that just kept us on an emotional rollercoaster," she says.

The Marana police kept the case open and they continued investigating the crime, but knowing who committed a crime is far from proving that person committed the crime. Mick and Karen had a number of meetings with the detective assigned to the case, but it was obvious the investigation was going nowhere. The police came by with a book of mug shots of possible suspects, an act that surprised the couple. This approach only added to their level of frustration and surprise. Other than the incidents with Fries, Mick and Karen hadn't experienced any confrontations with their neighbors, hired hands, other service providers or even any strangers. Mick says, "I kept telling Marana we know who did it. After a while the thought process should be obvious: what happened to us? Some imbecile came in there and destroyed our driveway. Well, excuse me, but who's mad at us? And what did he do for us? He did our driveway. So what was destroyed? Our driveway. Who thinks we owe him even though he did shoddy work? That's why I knew it was Fries."

Karen says, "I knew it was Todd. It had to be. I mean, who else?"

The lack of progress on the investigation added to the couple's stress. Fries was the only logical suspect. He hadn't left town. He was conducting his business as usual and living a normal life. If any of his employees had participated, they were also around for interrogation. Mick and Karen's lawn was littered with evidence. Their home was covered with it. Logic was on their side. What was the hold up?

As the investigation plodded on Mick's health took another nose dive. His doctor could no longer keep him off dialysis. "I had to spend three days a week of total hell and three days a week recuperating from it. What a life," he says. His health continued to decline despite the regular treatments. In the summer of 2009 his spine was rapidly deteriorating. He had to have neck surgery to repair the damage. The surgeons inserted steel plates between several disks so he could have continuing mobility with a minimum of pain. He could move, but those movements would have to be restricted and he would be required to use a neck brace.

Life at home was a mix of occasional normalcy broken by moments of uncertainty and fear. Imagine the stress of seeing a strange car or truck passing through the neighborhood and having to wonder if it's being driven by a neighbor's friend or hired hand or, perhaps, someone planning another attack on your house. Imagine what it's like going to bed wondering what kind of nightmare might awaken you in the middle of the night. Add to that the fear of the very real possibility that you might not even wake up because of – who knows what? That's not paranoia; that's living with an agonizing reality.

They moved to a house in another community, Omni Tucson National Resort in the foothills of the Santa Catalina Mountains southeast of Marana. This was an upscale gated community they believed would be a safe haven. "It was a nice place and we could afford it. And I felt a lot safer," Karen says. That expectation proved to be painfully and terrifyingly wrong, but for the moment they felt secure in their new home. By December they were moved, settled down and hoping for peace and quiet.

And then Mick suffered a ruptured appendix.

Karen says, "His diabetes was going haywire. He didn't look good. I was so depressed." The attack at Dove Mountain plus the strain of her husband's physical condition began to have a negative effect on her personality. "I was just very excitable. I didn't want to be with people, see people. At that time I think I actually hated people. I've always been a very outgoing, fun-loving person. But after all that had happened to us, I wasn't the fun-loving person I used to be."

While no one would consider her attitude a good approach to living, it played well into what came next. Mick says, "After the second attack, the FBI told us to lose all of our friends. No contact. Marana PD told us that." The authorities suggested the possibility that someone they knew was involved. They were urged to sever permanently all ties with their new friends and acquaintances. The situation was mentally and emotionally challenging. The man who had committed the crimes was living and working as if nothing had happened, yet the victims were living a life of ongoing and increasing hardship.

"Basically we were told, you know, cut off your life and start over," Mick says.

Then the Marana PD closed the case.

Mick and Karen were stunned. Matters deteriorated rapidly. Mick says, "I only had half a day a week that I felt normal because when you have dialysis you're shot that whole day. It takes the entire next day to recoup. Then you go back on dialysis again. She's depressed. I'm going crazy. Her mother is still telling us somebody's trying to kill us. Marana police tell us that there's nothing more they can do on the case because they don't know and they can't make anybody talk. No wonder I was so sick."

Karen says, "Anybody would be depressed. I had to be with Mick because of the dialysis. He had a lot of issues. I was the one who had to be strong. My dog, Roja, my pal, got me through a lot of hard times."

The dialysis wasn't going very well. Mick began to have blood pressure issues and he was constantly passing out. Physically, there were many things, even ordinary tasks, that his condition prevented him from doing. Mentally and emotionally he struggled to maintain a positive outlook and often he failed. "I didn't feel like giving up or anything like that. I was just totally drained – totally," he says.

"I thought he was dead one time. We had more than a few bad scares," Karen says.

One evening in July, Karen and her mother decided to go out and enjoy a meal at a restaurant in Tucson, the Blue Point Oyster Bar. They put thoughts of Todd Fries and what he was capable of doing out of their minds. They were due a relaxed evening free of fear and worry. Mick was feeling too ill to go along, so he stayed in with Roja and the television set.

Karen and her mother had a pleasant drive to the restaurant and were enjoying a relaxing evening. Then she looked away from the table and made eye contact with a man sitting at the bar a short distance away. He was Todd Fries. He recognized her and after a moment of surprise, stood up, and immediately left the bar. His departure was a relief, but only for a moment. "I didn't know if he might be waiting outside for me. When we left I checked the parking lot and everything to make sure he wasn't there. I didn't carry a gun at the time, so we were basically defenseless. I made sure no one was following me and then went home as fast as I could."

That's what being hunted can do to someone. A person can't even go out for a pleasant evening with friends or family without wondering who might be waiting in the dark parking lot or on a side street on the way home. The thought stays in the back of the mind – is the person doing these crazy things really crazy? What will that level of craziness drive that person to do?

The man wasn't in the parking lot, nor did they encounter him on the way home. For the moment they were rattled, but they felt safe inside the gated community. Sadly, that wasn't the last they would see of Todd Fries.

CHAPTER SIX

A WAKE UP CALL

W hen someone's kidneys are damaged and can no longer function, kidney dialysis is required if the person is to live. Dialysis is an artificial bodily process for the elimination of waste from the blood system. Although a major medical breakthrough, the process itself is simple. A catheter (flexible tube) is inserted into a vein and the blood is pumped out and processed through a filter. After it has been filtered the blood is circulated back into the patient. The process takes about three to four hours for each session. The process is truly a miracle of science, a life-saver if there ever was one, but it takes a toll on the human body. There's also a mental and emotional price as there is with many medical procedures.

August 2, 2009 – Mick had a tough Saturday at his dialysis session. In addition to the exhausted filtering process, he suffered from the surgery and was still wearing a neck brace. People who have been with patients during dialysis or who have seen it on television or in the movies might think that this seemingly simple process is as relaxing as an afternoon watching a television program or reading a book. After all, the patient just sits there while the machine does all the work. Few realize just how tiring the process becomes or how boring it is for the patient who is, after all, seriously ill. Mick found that he endured the dialysis, well but the sessions left him drained of energy. By the time he recovered from one session was time to head back for another. Essentially, he was on a rollercoaster of physical misery and discomfort while trying to remain upbeat and positive about making it through another trying day.

"Basically I had no life at all. That's how sick I was," he says.

They returned to their new home and settled in for the evening. Mick was exhausted as usual and quickly fell into a deep sleep. In the middle of the night Karen woke up. The house felt unusually warm, even for an Arizona evening. She got up around five a.m. and went into the living room to check on the house thermostat, which was by the front door. While examining the thermostat she noticed something through the window next to the door. The walk lights around the house illuminated something, a sight that kicked her in the gut and sent chills up her spine. The sidewalk and the yard was shiny and wet. Mounds of packing peanuts had been poured on the sidewalk. Other unidentifiable masses and lumps were mixed in with the slime. She could even smell the same foul stench of oil, feces and rot she had experienced at the Dove Mountain home.

Panicked, Karen screamed. "He did it again! He did it again!"

She ran, still screaming, to the bedroom and tried to wake up Mick. Exhausted from the trials of the day, he struggled toward consciousness. He was groggy, but her screaming brought him around. They rushed as quickly as possible to the front door. It would not open and appeared to be stuck. No matter how hard they pushed and struggled, the door would not budge. Each knew instinctively what had happened. What they didn't know was how serious the situation was. How far had Todd Fries pushed this thing this time? Was he out there, perhaps with a rifle or pistol? What would happen next?

Karen dialed 911, but was too emotionally overcharged to speak clearly with the operator. Mick took the phone. He told the operator his name, address and he described as best he could the nightmare unfolding around them. His breathing was heavy and his voice stressed as he fought to make the incredible sound credible, so they could get some help. The operator said "Why is your wife screaming 'He did it again?'" Apparently she thought at first she was taking a domestic abuse call and was addressing the abuser. Mick, controlling his emotions, told her quickly and coherently what he had first said. "You can call the Marana Police Department and verify this. It's the same issue we faced last year." He went on to describe the scene outside their front door. *How bad is this going to get,* he thought.

He kept the operator on the line, telling her he was walking to the garage to see if they could get outside that way. He wanted to keep her on the line in case some other nightmare presented itself. The operator was in every sense a real lifeline. About that short, but unnerving walk he says, "Now I'm thinking, okay let me go into the garage and see if I can open the garage door. That's logical because this same thing happened to us before. Maybe this time it will work. Maybe." He went through the kitchen, through the hallway, and into the garage, where he put his hand on the button to raise the garage door. The motor ground on, but the garage door would not open. What was later described as a "foam expanding seal" applied to the door prevented their escape. They were locked in – sealed in to be perfectly accurate. This was a repeat of what had happened at Dove Mountain.

"Damn it! It's the same thing. It's Todd Fries. He did it to us again."

Mick couldn't open the front door. He couldn't open the garage door. Worse when he returned to the front room and tried to open the windows in front of the house they were sealed shut with the same foaming seal. Moving around the house was made more difficult due to Mick's health. He had to use a walker to get around at that time. Moving quickly or turning suddenly could have caused serious and perhaps debilitating damage to his neck. Yet, speed was essential if they were to escape. At every turn, at every moment, the situation became worse.

He told all of this to the 911 operator as it was happening. She said that the department had just received a number of complaints from the neighborhood. A number of Pima County Sheriff's Dept. deputies had received reports of a strong chemical smell coming from the area near Magee Road and Jensen Drive and were responding. In fact, a couple of squad cars were already nearby, behind their home. She told them to leave the house by the back door and make their way to the officers and safety.

That's when Mick and Karen began to get an idea of just how bad, just how dangerous this latest episode was becoming. Escaping through the back door and back yard would be a challenge. Something was burning just outside the back door.

Mick says, "I saw a cloud billowing up. It looked like sparklers were shooting off within it. You couldn't tell what it was. And it smelled terrible. And we couldn't get around it because it was sparking, burning and smoking right there on the patio. They also heard an ominous crackling sound. All of this was between the doors and the gate in the back yard. It just smelled terrible." Mick says.

Karen says, "It was sizzling. It smelled like chlorine. Terrible. Strong."

One of their neighbors, Carly Riggs, was overcome by the fumes. He later told local ABC News affiliate KGUN that the gas had made him ill. He was making his morning coffee as the incident occurred. "All of a sudden I took a deep breath and I couldn't hardly breathe. It burned my lungs. If you've ever been in the military and went into tear gas, it was kind of like that. You just couldn't breathe. Every time you went to breathe it would cut your breath short."

In the federal trial the defense tried to claim that the events that evening were basically just pranks that got a little bit out of hand. But this prank is one that put neighbor Riggs in the hospital. Riggs lived across the street. He told KOLD news, "All I know is it was some kind of chlorine and I don't know what else. It was moving like a wall coming over the house. I'd left the back door open and got a bit whiff of whatever it was, gas or some type, and it burned. I got up and went outside." Riggs was taken by ambulance to a nearby hospital and didn't return home for seven hours. Later he said, "I hope they catch whoever done it, and I hope the let me get with him for five minutes."

Another neighbor, Roger Lake was interviewed by KOLD. He stated that the police took the threat very seriously very early on. "There was a policeman at the door with a gas mask on who said, 'grab a few things, get in our car, get out of here and evacuate.'"

The cloud was estimated to have been approximately 200 feet deep reaching 1000 feet into the air. The entire neighborhood had to be evacuated by HazMat teams. The local police, fire department, and sheriff's office clearly didn't think the incident fit in the category of a prank.

As their neighbors were making an escape, Mick told the 911 operator that he and Karen were trapped. She responded that she knew that, but the police were very close. She told them to look on the other side of the golf course greens, on the other side of the street. The police were there waiting for them.

Mick said, "You don't get it. We can't get out. We're trapped. I'm disabled. I'm in a neck brace; there's no way I can get over that wall." The wall was only three or four feet tall, but in his condition there was no way he could make it over on his own. A slip and a fall could cause serious injury or worse.

The 911 Operator encouraged them to make the effort. The police are very close. Just get over to them, she said.

Mick told her, "There's something burning in our back yard. It's right outside our back door. There's no way we can get out. Send those cops over here to help us. I'm telling you we're trapped. We're in trouble - now!"

The operator said the police wouldn't come over the wall and into their yard. They'd seen the cloud. They could smell the chlorine odor and they were afraid of exposure. They didn't have gas masks or HazMat protection and they had been told to stay where they were. Mick came to the surprising realization that help was nearby, but it wasn't coming to the rescue. He and Karen were on their own.

Mick says, "We couldn't get out the front door. We couldn't get out the garage door. And we were trapped by some foul-smelling burning something at our back door."

"I thought our house was going to blow up," Karen says.

"It may have only been five minutes, but at last the cops came over to help us. It seemed like it took them forever. They stayed on the other side of that wall, but they did help us and the dog get over," Mick says.

Karen says, "I don't know how we got through all of this. It was terrible and we really didn't know what was going on. Was this it? Was worse to come? What else did Fries have planned for us that night? We didn't know." For the moment they were just happy to be in good hands and out of immediate danger.

Things were chaotic. Mick and Karen were still in their pajamas. Pima County Sheriff's Deputies Atwell and Baird put on put on protective equipment and helped them evacuate the area. The police quickly took them about half a block away up a hill on the greens where they could see some of what was happening while they made their reports to the officers. Mick and Karen had no doubts as to who was responsible for the attack. They told the authorities that they were positive Todd Fries was the perpetrator. (When questioned during the investigation, Fries denied any involvement.) By this time emergency vehicles and patrol cars from several forces began to arrive. The HazMat unit, followed by the fire department, arrived.

"I watched these guys from the HazMat unit get into their suits. Nobody was in a hurry. Our house was on fire and nobody was in in a hurry. We didn't know what was burning in the back. All I remember is the smoke and the sparkles. The smoke was underneath the eave and curling around. There was a lot of smoke. It was a cloud of smoke." Later they learned that the burning substance had been set on fire in a bucket placed on their patio. Had escape through the front of the house been blocked so as to force them out the back and into the toxic cloud? All kinds of thoughts filled Mick's head. Something that hour earlier would have seemed insane had become a frightening reality in the here and now. They were shaken, in shock and aware that they were moving targets in their own home.

They were moved to the HazMat unit and were talking with the attendants when the question of just how dangerous the situation could be was answered. A loud boom followed by a thick cloud of black smoke burst from the front of the house.

"The house is on fire!" said Mick.

A moment passed, but the house didn't blaze. The flash, the boom and the black smoke all emanated from more buckets placed near the front door. Unsure of the nature of the explosion and what poison might be spreading through the air, the HazMat crew and the fire and police personnel were cautious. They moved very slowly to examine what was happening.

The terrifying situation was also frightening to some of the responders. It was certainly a major concern to all. The perpetrator had shown a complete disregard for the property, the health and well-being, and the lives of his victims. Everyone wondered if the incident was over or if some additional event was about to happen.

Deputy Sheriff Atwell upon approaching the scene noticed the strong chemical smell even through the closed windows of his vehicle. He reported that the buckets on the front drive was "popping and oozing" and emitting smoke. When he rushed to the back of the house he discovered another bucket oozing and popping and leaving a "smoke trail," which he said was "a little scary." While helping Mick and Karen escape he noticed "a massive grayish-yellow-white cloud" near the front of the residence. After helping with the rescue, Atwell put on a gas mask to assist with evacuating the neighborhood.

Deputy Christopher McCracken observed "a very dark cloud' that was "increasing in size dramatically" at the front of the house. Eventually, the cloud covered the entire cul de sac, he said. He also noticed the strong chlorine smell. McCracken also wore a gas mask when helping evacuate the neighborhood.

Pima County Sergeant Stephen Carpenter observed "a cloud of an enormous proportions that basically had enclosed and enveloped [the] whole area" near the residence. He also noticed that the cloud moved slowly, spreading into other parts of the neighborhood. As Carpenter approached the Levine's home his "throat started to burn, [his] eyes burned. The skin on [his] face burned" and he experienced difficulty breathing.

A member of the fire district's hazardous material unit, Bert Rucker, stopped before reaching the house when he saw a dense cloud "approximately 30 feet high, 40 feet wide, and several hundred feet long, and hanging close to the ground."

A firefighter, Levi Cranford, noticed the smoking bucket behind the home. He put on a protective suit and entered the home with atmospheric measuring equipment. Conditions inside the residence did not indicate the presence of chlorine, but readings inside the garage showed levels higher than the recommended level that any person should be in unless protected by a Level A environmental suit.

Sergeant Christopher Rogers, a Pima County Sheriff's Department bomb technician, confirmed that report. Using a robot equipped with chemical detection devices he reported a positive reading for chlorine near the garage. He also stated that the use of a sealed bucket would intensify the dispersion of chlorine gas as the substance exploded. He further stated that the burning substances had the great potential to cause serious physical injury or death.

Heath Evans, Battalion Chief on the scene, reported a chemical cloud approximately 1000 feet long, 100 feet high, and about 200 feet deep. It was "one big solid mass hanging over the neighborhood" that was impossible to see through. He tracked the cloud for about an hour as it floated to the Santa Cruz River approximately three and a half miles distant.

Dr. Frank Walter, a medical toxicologist and emergency medical technician, later testified that chlorine gas is toxic and can be immediately dangerous to life and health of persons exposed to it.

In addition to the two devices containing materials used to produce the gas, deputies Atwell and Baird found the bodies of a cat, coyote, rabbit and numerous woodpeckers scattered around the Levine's house. Pima County detective Alexander Tisch found a black day planner containing a driver's license for Michele Fuentes, business cards for Debbie's Cleaning Service, and a check from Fuentes made out to Karen Levine. The check had a notation "refund customer unhappy." Later, a latent fingerprint belonging to Fries was found on that check.

Mick and Karen were taken up the hill and put in a van, a mobile unit that had come up from Tucson. They were safe, but still trapped by confusion, frustration and anger. "He did it again!" A couple of hours passed. The home never caught fire and the police and firemen went through the property looking for any more explosive devices and checking for damage. Again the damage estimates were more than $10,000. Mick complained that he needed to get back into the house to get his medication, especially his insulin. They were told it was impossible at that time. They were kept at the van until someone from the fire department showed up. He said they would be taken to a hospital for an examination.

They were put in an ambulance together and as the ambulance drove away they got a good look at the scene. Emergency, first responder and other official cars and vans lined the road. Police and fire department officials walked in and around their home. Smoke hung in the heavy morning air. Worried and confused neighbors watched from the safety of their own homes. An evacuation was in progress. It was a dark scene of chaos. The effort to make sense of the chaos and to bring justice to the Levines would involve the Northwest Fire Department, the Marana Police Department, the Tucson Police Department, the Pima County Sheriff's Department, and the Federal Bureau of Investigation.

In a very real way, that night of chaos was a glance into the chaos that would dominate the next eight years of their lives.

CHAPTER SEVEN

WE GOTTA GET OUT OF THIS PLACE

When they arrived at Tucson's Northwest Hospital, the attendants made sure that Mick was first into the emergency room. Both victims were eventually checked out from head to toe and Mick was able to get the medication he needed. Each was still in a mild state of shock. They were very confused by the violence that had occurred, the speed of it all, and the frantic rush to safety. The "what next" question was always on their minds.

The first time Mick and Karen knew of an FBI interest in their situation was when two agents full of questions showed up at the hospital. Bureau interest was somewhat confusing because the first incident back at Dove Mountain had not been classified as a hate crime. *Why are these guys here,* thought Mick. As far as the two victims were concerned they knew precisely who had attacked them and that the incident didn't fit the government's definition of a hate crime. They believed that the attack was a little bit about money and a lot about revenge or some kind of "payback."

The FBI agents conducted the interviews separately. Mick and Karen repeated their story and kept telling the agents that they knew who committed the crimes. Separately and in their own words they described the earlier incidents and the events leading up to all the troubles. The agents then switched places and conducted the interviews again. Mick's interview did not go smoothly.

The agent opened with, "Why don't you like Hispanic people?"

The question floored Mick. "I looked at him and says, "What! Todd Fries isn't Hispanic."

"Mr. Levine, you told the Marana police that one of the people who could have done this was Hispanic, didn't you?"

"No. That's not what I told them. They asked me if I had any conflicts with contractors and I told them one of the conflicts was with a Hispanic. I also told them I didn't think he was smart enough to do this."

"Well, then, why don't you like Hispanic people?"

Perhaps the agent was using an unusual investigative technique, but Mick felt the man was trying to use the questions to mold Mick's answers into a predetermined resolution. Mick responded with barely suppressed emotion, "Number one, my sister-in-law is Hispanic. And number two my best friend is Hispanic. So, don't tell me I don't like Hispanic people. I don't like *you*. But I have nothing against Hispanic people."

Today, Mick says, "I was really mad at this guy. He kept on with this Hispanic… Hispanic… Hispanic. I found out later they asked Karen the same thing. We kept telling them the case had nothing to do with Hispanics. Todd Fries did it."

Later on one of the agents came by and told them the hospital would release them soon. Obviously they couldn't return home, so the agent asked where they would be staying. They decided to stay with Karen's mother. The agent left saying that the bureau would be in touch. On the way to the house they stopped and purchased some clothes.

They weren't allowed back into their house until about 11 o'clock at night. The police, firemen, HazMat team members and others were still at work assessing the damage, looking for clues, and processing the scene. They had been there since five a.m. Neither Mick nor Karen had a clue as to how things were developing. The officers in charge did agree to let them back in the house to grab Mick's medication and a few other things. But they were only allowed ten minutes inside. Their home was still a crime scene under active investigation.

Back in the house a lot of people were looking very busy. Big fans blew loudly and with force enough to clear the house of smoke and, hopefully, any toxic fumes. The police and fire department personnel had been just as frustrated by the sealed front door trying to get in as had been Mick and Karen in trying to get out. They broke it down to gain entrance.

The next day Mick and Karen were allowed back in to their home. Only then in the light of day could they see all that had happened. "The house was a total disaster," Karen says. The authorities had even brought in an air quality control expert from Phoenix to make sure the air was safe enough to breathe. The large air-mover fans were still blowing. Cables were all strewn all over the house. A big window in Mick's office had been blown out and shattered. There was a large hole in the garage door. Burn marks also scarred the door. Their SUV was damaged as was Mick's prize Corvette, which had paint damage all over it. It looked like a total loss.

The physical damage to their home from the initial incident through the escape and during the subsequent investigations made the couple ill at heart and mind.

Mick says, "That's when we noticed the graffiti, different kinds of graffiti. I think there was one swastika, too. We heard that the spray painted signs were representative of Mexican Mafia graffiti. That was painted all over the house. Except that a friend of mine says, it's not the Mexican Mafia. I asked him why and he says that whoever spray painted those signs didn't spell it right. It's not the Mexican Mafia. The graffiti is not correct he told me."

As in the earlier incident in Dove Mountain, the yard had been thoroughly and disgustingly trashed. Spread throughout the front driveway, sidewalk and the walkway leading to the front door was a thick, viscous, slimly material which appeared to be a combination of paint and motor oil coating a mass of packing peanuts. The bodies of the dead animals were still present. *What kind of mind could even conceive of something like this,* he wondered.

Mick's brother came over and helped with the cleanup. Karen was at times horrified and at times sick over what had been done to her beautiful home. "It was another total mess. I had to call different clean up services all over again to clean up and repair the damage to the garage door. It was all very time consuming and expensive. Worst of all we missed the Jewish High Holy Days of Rosh Hashanah and Yom Kippur because we had to deal with the awful situation."

Both sides of the cul de sac were lined with a series of lights that come on automatically at dusk. These would have spotlighted anyone sneaking around the property at night. After a brief investigation they discovered that the light bulbs were loose. The subsequent darkness after sundown allowed the perpetrator to get in and attack the house and its occupants in the darkness. The attack had been well-planned and executed.

The FBI continued to question the couple, but no one in authority at the local, county, state or federal level commented on the investigation or kept them in the loop on what was happening. The loop started becoming convoluted two days after the incident. According to FBI Agent Brian Nowak, a person purporting to be Michele Fuentes contacted the FBI in Tucson claiming to have important information regarding the incident. The caller spoke with FBI Agent John Edwards and said that when she had worked for the Levines as a domestic Mr. Levine had asked her to 'engage in sex acts.' She told the FBI she had refused and had informed Mrs. Levine of the harassment. The caller also stated that the Levines had refused to pay her for her cleaning services and that Mrs. Levine threatened to report her to immigration services. She added that she had informed her cousin, Joaquin Contreras-Navarette about the incidents at the Levine household. She stated that Navarette was an 'extremely violent' person who had admitted to stealing a large amount of chlorine tablets and placing them in buckets around the Levines' residence. Out of the blue a tip comes in that apparently ties all the investigative leads into a nice, tidy package.

Case solved.

Nowak didn't believe the call tied things up as nicely as the caller intended. Although the caller said she was a Mexican national, she spoke perfect English. Also, Agent Edwards immediately suspected the caller was a man pretending to sound like a female. He believed the caller was using a "spoofcard," an electronic device that alters the caller's voice. The unit also hides the caller's phone number during the call rendering the call untraceable. Spoofcards are legal if used properly and are readily available for purchase. Fries, or anyone else, could have easily purchased one.

Mick's response to the allegation was understandably explosive, "And my statement back was, 'Wait a minute! First of all I don't know who this is. Second, we didn't have a maid at Tucson National. Third of all, I'm doing dialysis. I'm in a neck brace. I have no life whatsoever. I'm not awake most of the time. This person told the FBI 'My cousin did it because I refused to have oral sex with Mr. Levine and Mrs. Levine threw me out and wouldn't pay me.' That's ridiculous in so many ways. Absolutely ridiculous."

Edwards was able to trace the "Fuentes" call to the Avalon Rehabilitation Center where employees had noticed an unauthorized person on the floor from which that call had been made. The unknown man had entered from a stairwell, walked to a computer terminal where there was a phone, used the phone and then left. When agents showed her a photograph of Fries' driver's license, she identified Fries as the unauthorized person she had seen. Further investigation revealed the phone had been used to make a call to the local FBI office. Fries' latent fingerprint was recovered from the phone used to make that call.

The real Michele Fuentes was found. She testified at trial that her purse had been stolen in 2007 while she was attending college. It had contained her driver's license, social security card, checks, and her day planner. She was shown the check she had supposedly written. The check was not in her handwriting, she said. Furthermore, she had never worked at a cleaning service and did not know anyone named Joaquin Navarette. Fuentes would testify that she didn't know the Levines, had never heard of them, and had never been to their home.

A wallet belonging to a Kaylin Hovey and containing a driver's license and business cards had been found in the Levine's front yard after the 2008 attack. The FBI located Ms. Hovey who identified the license and other items, but not the wallet. Agents later learned that the wallet had been stolen in October, 2005. Hovey said that she was in a car accident in October, 2005 and that when she was in the hospital her wallet disappeared from her purse.

Nowak kept them informed as best he could under the conditions of a criminal investigation. Confidential sources provided information concerning Fries' frequent use of a laptop and that he had stockpiled "buckets, used oil, feces and dead animals" at his home for the purpose of future attacks.

The investigation continued to confirm what Karen and Mick already knew. Fries had for some time plotted and eventually executed a plan of attack against them. For example, during the federal and state trials a former employee of Burns Power Washing, Edward Trujillo, testified that when Fries received the Levine's cancelled check he became very upset and that "He wanted to make [the Levines] pay for not paying him." He said Fries then began collecting materials for his attack, materials that included motor oil. He also said Fries asked his employees to defecate in buckets so that he could use the mess as part of his payback scheme. It is from Trujillo's testimony that the court learned of Fries name his revenge – "the Levine Project." He stated that Fries planned to pour the oil and feces over the targeted yard, spray paint the house, and to place dead animals on the grounds. He added that Fries had called Mick to thank him for the payment just to throw them off the track so he would suspect others of the attack.

The net grew tighter in 2009 as more employees were brought into the investigation of the Levine 09 Project. Austreberto "Ray" Montiel would later testify as to Fries' anger over the cancelled check, and to the instructions to the employees to collect motor oil and dead animals. His boss did not hide the fact that these and other materials would be used against Mick and Karen Levine. He even offered Montiel $100 to help in vandalizing the Levine's property, but the man refused. Montiel, who had worked for Burns Power Washing from 2006 – 2009, observed both of Fries' Levine projects. He said his boss had told him he had located the home where the Levines were living by researching the Internet. He was present when Fries and another employee drove to the Omni Tucson National Golf Course, left the car, and walked over to look at the property where the Levines lived. About a week prior to the 2009 incident Montiel says he was power-washing his truck when he looked to his right and saw Fries and another employee running away from another vehicle where a gray-white plume rose into the air.

As with David Trujillo, Montiel quit Burns Power Washing after he heard about the incident.

Fries also related conversations with another employee, Dan Jordan, who had been instructed to collect road kill for the "Levine 09 Project" in 2008. He added that on Halloween night Fries and Jordan discussed vandalizing the home that evening, perhaps hoping that the attack would be attributed to pranksters getting out of hand. Montiel said that Fries bragged about the attack stating that he had spray painted swastikas to give the impression that the event was a hate crime and not related to payback over a business deal gone sour. Fries also admitted to leaving false clues at the scene, specifically someone else's identification.

As the investigation slowly became stronger, so did the stress and strain on Mick and Karen Levine. Karen says, "We had multiple interviews with the FBI agents. We were told we would have to move again and quickly. Worst of all they told us we couldn't let anyone know where we were." They felt that Brian Nowak, who was the agent in charge, was the nicer of the two agents.

Nowak told them, "You have to avoid all contact with anyone you know. You find a place, you move, how you do it I don't care, you let us know where you are." Despite the level of the events that had already occurred, his words were sobering. Mick says, "We had to cut ourselves off from everybody and everything. They said and we shouldn't waste any time doing it."

Mick remembered a song from the sixties by a British group called The Animals. It was called *We Gotta Get Out of This Place.* There's a line in that song, "Girl, there's a better life for me and you." For Mick and Karen Levine that better life was a long way off.

CHAPTER EIGHT

LIVING GHOSTS

Karen and Mick entered a long period marked by confusion, doubt and very real and ongoing fear. During the lengthy time the local and federal authorities investigated the case a man responsible for terrible acts was free. His calculated actions had proven that he was a danger to life and property, that he could take action without regard to the consequences. He was free to act again. Was he already planning another and perhaps more life-threatening incident? If he attacked again would they be as fortunate as the last time and be able to escape alive and unhurt? If he struck a third time, would Mick and Karen survive? The guilty walked free while the innocent victims were in a very real sense prisoners.

Imagine living in a world of not-knowing. That strange truck driving through the neighborhood – was it driven by someone just passing through or was it Todd Fries checking them out for another strike? Is the man walking down the street a door-to-door salesman or someone with sinister motives, perhaps an employee of Burns Power Washing checking them out? How about that hang-up telephone call – a miss-dial or someone calling to see if they're home? Such feelings at first might seem paranoid to the average citizen. But the average citizen has never had his yard covered in filth, refuse and dead animals. The average citizen hasn't had his house spray painted with swastikas or gang-related graffiti. And the average citizen hasn't been sealed in his house and his life threatened by chlorine gas. Such things give a couple a different perspective on the everyday occurrences of normal life.

The investigation advanced slowly. The FBI was involved automatically. In addition to the hate crime aspect of the crime, the canisters that produced the chlorine gas fit the legal definition of a chemical bomb according to the Patriot Act. The FBI interviews helped control some of those fears. Karen liked the approach and the reassurances of agent Brian Nowak. She says, "Brian was very good and I felt safe because he was handling this case. I didn't feel like there'd be any repercussions from any of Fries' friends or associates. I just felt pretty safe when I was talking to him." Mick had similar impressions. "My interview with Brian was short, but he was hearing what I was saying about Todd Fries. That I knew it was Todd Fries. Please go after him. Whatever it takes, I said."

Nowak knew better than most the scope and complexity of such an investigation. "There were a lot of challenges. Whenever you deal with a Weapon of Mass Destruction (WMD) or a chemical weapon there are a lot of challenges with collection and preservation of evidence. There's also a lot of unique challenges because of the size of the incident. The initial incident that we responded to in 2009, that lasted 18 hours in a day and involved literally hundreds of people at the site, including the two bomb squads, a complete HazMat team, almost a whole fire department, three or four separate police departments along with the FBI," he says.

The FBI or the county or local authorities can't be around 24/7. People who are on-guard all the time still have to sleep. And a couple wary of virtually everything still has to go out into the community to buy food, shop and take care of day-to-day business. At that time and in that place real danger to life and limb could be just around the next corner, through the next door, or down the next street. Regardless of how they felt during the interviews, Mick and Karen still had to live in the world of not-knowing.

Karen says, "It was terrible. I didn't wear makeup. I wore a baseball cap when I went out – you know, like a movie star with sunglasses to hide her identity. I wore terrible clothes. I didn't feel like getting dressed. When we moved from Tucson National, the house we were staying in was very depressing. It wasn't very cheery and there were no windows except in the back." The design of the house, although only a temporary residence, only added to their sense of isolation.

Before the incidents they had enjoyed an outgoing lifestyle. Afterwards they became a stay-at-home couple. They no longer went out for dinner or entertainment. Fridays and Saturdays never seemed like days off and were really just two more days to get through. "It was like we had no life. On New Year's Eve we didn't even go out that year. We just stayed in and made the best of it."

Mick fought a continuing battle with depression. The combination of his physical condition with the mental stress of being hunted took its toll on a day-to-day and hour-by-hour basis. Karen hates guns, but he insisted that she get one and get a concealed carry permit. "I didn't feel she was safe. And we didn't know if, when or how Fries might be coming at us again."

Karen says," I was scared. When I did go out with my mom, I was nervous driving home by myself. Is he following me? Does he know where we live now? Will he be waiting when I get home? He didn't kill me, but now I was afraid I was going to get killed. I was afraid to go to a mall. I was always on my guard."

They had followed the authorities' suggestion and had cut off all contact with friends, neighbors and associates. The only person Karen could confide in was her mother. "My mother got me through this. And my dog." Today, long after the investigations and the trials, the effects of those years linger. "I always feel lonely. I still feel lonely. I'm just taking each day at a time. The thing is still here. We're still going through it. There's sentencing, hearings, it's all still with me," Karen says.

They found a new home in a part of Tucson known as Sabino Canyon which is located next to the Coronado National Forest. It's a beautiful place and an ideal location for a beautiful life. Of course, how beautiful can life be for a couple living under a constant threat? Beautiful is a relative term when someone is always looking over his or her shoulders.

These are the kinds of thoughts that plague people under the constant threat of attack. They're inevitable and unending. Still, the new home gave them some new hope. "Mick says, "The house had a high wall around it. And a front and back gates that were locked. We figured, okay maybe we'll be safe here."

Eventually the interviews ended. The Marana police dropped out of the investigation, followed soon by Pima County and the City of Tucson. Due to the violation of the Patriot Act, the FBI took control of the investigation. More interviews followed and Mick and Karen had to cover the same territory and answer the same questions again.

Mick's health continued to deteriorate. He was on dialysis. On April 12, 2010 he needed kidney and pancreas transplants. He has Type o-blood a rare blood type which added to the challenge. Fortunately, they got a phone call in the middle of the night that brought immediate hope. The hospital had organs matching his blood type, but they had to act within 48 hours. Mick went "under the knife" right away. The surgery went well, but recovery took about six months for Mick "to feel like a human being again." Karen says of that part of the experience, "Without my dog Roja's unconditional love and the support I got from my mom I don't think I would have made it."

Meanwhile, the legal operations continued. Nowak says of that time, "The important factor to take away from that is that federal law enforcement works with their local law enforcement, works together with the local fire department, and the EMS to really bring together a unified command presence at the site of a major incident like that. That worked very well. I immediately met with the HazMat, fire department coordinator, local law enforcement. We all really worked together in a unified command setting to develop an investigative plan of action and obviously deal with the public safety issues during the initial incident because we did have a chemical cloud release."

Even a well-managed investigation can appear chaotic to an outsider, especially if legitimate rules of investigation require that the principles in the case remain outside the loop on what is happening. Mick says, "We were going nuts. They were telling us this and that is going on. Here's what we're doing. It's 2010 by then, the second year of living like this for us and Todd Fries still hasn't been arrested. It's taking forever and meanwhile we're living like prisoners in our own house," Mick says. In addition to moving to a new home, they were told not go any place, not to see anyone, not to do anything that might draw attention to them. They had to get rid of their cars, including his classic Corvette. "Because we were told don't keep anything that you now have. Don't go anyplace. Don't see anybody. Don't have a life. Become a ghost and that's what we were – ghosts."

The couple built up a good relationship with Agent Novak and found some comfort and confidence in the way he was handling the case.

Tucson is a large town, but in many ways a small community wherein lies much of its charm. Casual and unexpected encounters with friends are common when out at about. The same can be says for encounters of a more serious nature. Mick was running an errand one day when he saw Todd Fries' truck. It was unmistakable – a three-color paint job with the words Burns Power Washing on the side. Mick immediately called Agent Nowak.

"I called Brian and said Todd is next to me. Brian says, 'Does he see you?' And I said, I don't think so because he doesn't know the car I'm driving. Brian then says for me to make a left turn – quickly. That told me that there was no question about it. They knew Todd had done it. He told me to take a lot of turns and to call him when I got home. And to make sure that nobody followed me home."

The situation became more complicated as the investigation continued. Apparently Fries had gone after other people in a similar hostile manner. Mick and Karen got a phone call at the house. The Caller ID read Marguerite Brown. They had no idea who this woman was or what she wanted. She asked if the man on the line was Myles Levine and Mick responded in the affirmative. She said that she had acquired their phone number from the Tucson Police Department. The woman sounded sincere, but considering the nature of what had happened to the Levines what did that really mean – if anything?

Mick was skeptical. "I'm thinking there's no way in hell you got my name from the Tucson PD. But I didn't say anything and I let her keep on talking." Brown asked if he had any business contact with Burns Power Washing. He asked her why she had asked that question. She said that she had an issue at her house and had just hired a contractor. The police had told her that Mick and Karen Levine had had the same type of issue with the same man and company. "I said, Miss Brown I don't know who you are. You don't know me. I'm involved in an ongoing investigation and I can' tell you anything about it," Mick said.

He hung up the phone and called Nowak who said the woman was legitimate. Mick wanted to know why he had given the woman their unlisted phone number. Nowak says he hadn't shared that information, but that she was legitimate. He speculating that the city or county police may have given the phone number to her. He added that Brown had just experienced something like what the Levines had experienced with Burns Power Washing.

Karen called the authorities regularly, especially Nowak. The response was as expected. They were building a solid case and needed to make sure all the facts were in, examined and evaluated for trial. That's understandable in any case, but this case was special. It was the first of its kind. The government wanted to tie the guilty party to the crime so thoroughly that it would be a "no brainer" case.

Their case was the first of its kind. They wanted to cover completely every possible detail to make sure that an arrest would go through without complications and when the case went to court it would be solid. Karen says, "That was the most aggravating... not arresting him. It took two years to arrest him. I called Brian at least twice a week. I stayed on him, but he kept reminding me that they had to go through proper channels and assemble an airtight case. I don't even think that if Marguerite Brown hadn't have had that incident things would have happened as fast as they did."

"They wouldn't have arrested him if he hadn't done it to her twice," Mick says.

Marguerite Brown had contracted with Burns Power Washing in 2010 after a referral from a Sherman Williams representative. She contracted the company to clean her driveway and part of her back porch area. She also wanted to have her garage sealed with an epoxy sealer. They agreed to a standard payment plan: half in advance and a half upon completion payment schedule.

She was dissatisfied with the quality of the job. She noted that the workmen had moved her furniture and cabinets back onto the porch before the paint had properly dried. When she moved the furniture later the epoxy scraped off and ruined some of her furniture.

AT 7:30 a.m. on May 31 Brown called the Pima County Sheriff's Office to report a significant amount of vandalism to her Tucson residence. The door handles of her Jeep and of her daughter's red Volvo had been covered with epoxy glue. Epoxy had also been used to seal over the windows and windshield wiper blades and had even been poured into the gas tank. Not too long after the incident, Brown's daughter, Anna, was at the residence when someone called to offer apologies for the incident. The voice sounded like a woman. The caller said her son was responsible. Caller ID and a reverse telephone search produced the name provided. The police followed up only to discover that the caller didn't live at that address and that the phone was no longer in use. The agents certainly recognized a familiar pattern, but for legal and logical reasons Mick and Karen were kept out of the loop.

Brown was attacked again in 2011. She woke up one morning to find motor oil, epoxy, and packing peanuts scattered all over her yard. An employee of Burns Power Washing, Matt Wallenmeyer, would later testify that he remembered how Fries had treated Brown and that Fries was unhappy with Brown withholding the second payment

Deputies responded and found that two of her vehicles and her driveway had been damaged with glue and acid, causing more than $2,000 in damage. Brown suspected Fries because she had had an argument with him about some work his company had done for her. She was dissatisfied with the quality of that work. She refused to make the final half-payment until the damage was repaired. Another woman had stood up to the owner of Burns Power Washing and was paying a similar price in harassment.

As with the situation with Mick and Karen, the harassment escalated. The Pima County Sheriff's was called out on April 28, 2011 to the Brown home. Officers found that more oil had been poured on her driveway and block wall. Feces and a dead lizard had also been left on the property. The officers also found an ID card belonging to a Jina Parks. Again, an apparently legitimate clue had been left at the scene of the crime.

What was coming next? That question surely concerned the authorities as much as it concerned Brown. Property had already been destroyed. Innocent lives had been put at risk. An entire neighborhood had been evacuated. If things progressed to a higher level of revenge, truly what terror could possibly be next?

Months passed as Mick and Karen continued to live "inside the walls." Eventually they received a phone call from Beverly Anderson, a federal prosecutor assigned to the case. She says, "We're going to arrest Todd Fries on Friday afternoon. We want to make sure he can't get out of jail until Monday because we want to serve a warrant on his home. I just wanted to let you know."

Mick says, "I believe if Fries hadn't had done it to Margarite Brown the second time he would have still been on the street. I think she called me just to let us know they were going to arrest him because they knew how upset we were. I think the feds put on a very good case. They had everything in order. The only thing I didn't like about the federal trial was that they waited so long to arrest him before the trial. They knew it was him a couple of years before they arrested him," Mick says.

Agent Nowak called Karen that same day. "He says, 'Guess what, Karen?' It was May 13, 2011. Brian said, 'I'm on my way to arrest him.' I said, 'Can I come?' He said, 'I don't think that's a good idea.' But he said there were 30 squad cars lined up in front of his house. This was a big thing."

The FBI, the Marana PD, and the Pima County Sheriff's Office investigated the crimes against the Levines and Ms. Brown. Their research led the teams to believe that Fries was responsible for all of the attacks. They obtained a search warrant for Fries' residence on May 13, 2011. A search of his house in the 5300 block of West El Camino del Cerro uncovered evidence linking him directly to those attacks. One of the items seized included written material. Fries hand purchased a how-to-get-even book titled *The Encyclopedia of Revenge*. The book's promotional copy states: *Over 1000 revenge techniques enable anyone "falling down" to fight back, whether it's against the neighborhood bully, a corporate giant, or anyone in between. Also included are sections on the philosophy of revenge, using common sense, classic quotations and staying safe in covert operations. An appendix is full of resources for further study. Here's an emporium of revenge-something for everyone.* The techniques described include text on how to produce, make or manufacture bombs, chemical weapons or destructive devises. This book and many like it are readily available online and at certain book outlets. Karen says, "That proved he had all this planned out in advance. These plans were in his head, so he bought these revenge books so he could get even with us."

The authorities also seized Fries' laptop and computer equipment. During the search of one of the bedrooms agents also found 24 homemade cylindrical or spherical explosive devices containing a low-explosive main change. Three devices contained copper-plated metal balls for use as added fragmentation. There could only be one used for such devices and that would be to hurt or possibly kill human beings.

One of the most curious and most disgusting finds was a collection of dead woodpeckers that had been abused. They were identical to the woodpeckers dumped at the Levine's home in the first attack at Dove Mountain. In the words of Assistant Attorney Sterling Struckmeyer at a later trial, the dead birds had been strung up "almost like they're in a wreath hanging from the defendant's tree." The birds were tied with yellow zip ties exactly as were the birds used in the attacks on the Levines' property. Animal cruelty would become an issue at trial. Later Fries would acknowledge killing the birds claiming that they had been a constant nuisance at his home. He claimed to have tried various options, but when none worked he became "frustrated and anxious" and resorted to killing them.

They also found identification belonging to a Linda Mott.

Apparently Fries actions concerned at least one of his neighbors. In a local news report a neighbor of eight years, Sparky Waters, stated that he was wary of Fries and had put up a wall between their properties for that reason. He is reported to have said, "I didn't have that wall up the whole time, and he used to walk through here, I put that wall up because of him."

Mick says, "I wanted to say thank God. It had taken three years and they're finally going to arrest him." The arrest was a big event for the Tucson news media and received coverage on all the local television stations and in the newspapers.

Mick and Karen went to court to observe the proceeding. The judge declared that Fries was a menace to the Levines and to the community at large and that he wasn't going anywhere as a free man. Bail was denied. Todd Fries was now living "behind the walls."

The FBI/Phoenix Division issued a news release about the arrest stating in part, "A federal grand jury returned a two-count indictment today against Todd Russell Fries, aka Todd Burns, of Tucson, for allegedly producing and using chemical weapons…. Fries, 48, faces felony charges of prohibition against chemical weapons…." U.S. Attorney Dennis K. Burke is quoted, "This defendant developed and executed a chlorine gas attack that impacted an entire neighborhood and had the potential to cause tremendous harm and fear." The release noted that the crime carried a penalty of prison time, a $250,000 fine, or both. Assistant U.S. Attorney Beverley K. Anderson would be handling the case.

Todd Fries was going to jail to face charges in a federal court. For Karen and Mick Levine this was at last a step in the right direction, but it was only a first step on a long and complicated journey.

CHAPTER NINE

"LEVINE 09" BECOMES A FEDERAL CASE

"**A**re you going to sue my client?"

*The question was posed to Mick by Richard Bock, the attorney for Todd Fries. Bock, a licensed attorney for more than 40 years, specialized in criminal defense, DUI and DWI, sex crime, federal crime, and juvenile law. He had the unenviable challenge of defending a client facing an enormous amount of evidence against him.

Mick says, "Why would he ask me that? I told him that the state requires me to because they paid for a lot of stuff because of him and that was the agreement. If Fries was found guilty we would sue him so they could recoup their money. I didn't think he had any right asking me that. It was a stupid question. In the state trial he started in the same way. He came up with this nonsense about, well, "You taught ethics to car dealers didn't you?" I said yes and I also tried to teach ethics to lawyers and it didn't work. He would ask me questions I didn't think were appropriate and that he should be asking himself the same questions." Perhaps the questions were part of a defense strategy. One observer to one of the trials described the attorney's approach as "throwing everything against the wall hoping something will stick."

Todd Fries called his first attack on Mick and Karen "the Levine Project" and his second, "Levine 09." His "Levine 09" project became a federal case in *The United States of America vs. Todd Russell Fries, AKA Todd Burns.* U.S. District Judge Cindy K. Jorgenson presided. The trial lasted three weeks, which sounds like a reasonably short period of time. It is unless you're in the unenviable position of reliving a terrifying experience that ruined your home, your lifestyle, and could have easily cost you your life.

One of the most interesting, and frustrating, elements of trial preparation for Mick and Karen was the fact that they were basically kept "out of the loop." Mick says, "The federal trial was interesting. We talked to them about what we had been through, but I think what was interesting is that we didn't know anything at all about what they were doing. We knew nothing about it. We weren't even allowed to be there for the opening statements." Keeping Mick and Karen in the dark was part of a trial strategy. Mick asked about that approach. "They said, 'We don't want anyone coming back and saying that your testimony was tainted because you knew what was happening.' So, we knew nothing. We knew nothing about the background of what they knew or what they found out or what they proved what happened to us or even how they arrested him."

This was the first case tried under a new law and the authorities were taking absolutely no chances that their case would fail. They were committed to presenting an airtight case that would not be lost on appeal. That's admirable, but those necessary steps placed incredible personal burdens on the innocent victims in that case.

One of the worst aspects of being out of the loop is the inescapable feeling of what might happen next. Will the perpetrator strike again before he's brought to justice? Will either one of us or both of us live to see justice prevail? Is Fries or one of his friends or associates lurking around the next corner? They knew who committed the crimes and had clearly identified him, yet nothing seemed to be happening.

One day Mick decided to test the waters to see what was really going on – if anything serious was going on. He called agent Nowak and said, "Brian, I was just driving next to Todd in his truck. I don't know if he saw me or not. He doesn't know this car. What should I do? That's when he told me to make a quick left turn and drive all over and make sure he doesn't follow me. Right then I knew that they knew he did it. But that was a long time before they arrested him. That really put the damper on it for me."

Karen struggled perhaps more from the lack of information. She called Nowak frequently "I didn't give up. I was on it. I wanted to get this guy.

Except for that one time when my mom and I saw him at the oyster bar, I never saw him after he did it to us, but then again we didn't go out much."

They were told to stay in and remain out of sight as much as possible. Imagine the effect of that lifestyle – knowing the perpetrator is out and about and free as a bird while you're in an emotional prison. They lived in a house with high walls, which added to the feeling that they were the ones in jail, not the guilty party. "It was terrible," Karen says.

Mick's health continued to be a serious problem. "When you're told by the FBI that you have to disappear and have no contact with anybody you know, that you can no longer do anything, it affects every part of your life. I really think I wouldn't have gone through all those health problems if it had not been for the stress of those trials."

Karen says, "They wanted so much evidence against him that they were not going to lose this case because we were told they had never tried anybody under this section of the law before. From what they told me, the bombing section of the law had never been to court because they tied it into the terrorist act. That's why they wanted it airtight."

Sidebar

A note to the reader: Mick and Karen use the term "bomb" in their retelling of their struggle. Emotionally, that's correct, but legally the term is inaccurate. As FBI Agent Nowak stated, "It wasn't a bomb. It was a chemical weapon. That was the chemical weapon device. When we talk about that it was the combining of two or three chemicals to then release a toxic cloud and chemical weapon in the line of a chlorine dispersion device and toxic gas."

For reasons of convenience and to reinforce the emotional strain on the victims, the term "bomb" will be used as stated in all quotations from Mick and Karen.

End Sidebar

Stated simply, the federal trial revolved around two basic themes: the chemical weapon that released the chlorine gas and Fries' lying to federal official. The explosive charges found during an executed search warrant of Fries' home brought in the element of explosive devices.

As agent Nowak put it, "The federal trial, the main nexus of that was the chemical weapons charge – the illegal use of a chemical weapon. The second federal trial involved the explosives charges or the homemade IEDs and the lying to a federal office."

Although the various federal statutes assign responsibility for the investigation of chemical devices, bombs, firearms and so on to different agencies such as the FBI or the ATF, the FBI had jurisdiction over this case.

A chemical weapon uses a toxic chemical or chemicals used to produce a toxic chemical for illegal purposes; a munition or device designed to cause physical harm or death; and equipment designed for use in the munition or device. A toxic chemical is defined as a chemical that can cause death, temporary incapacitation, or permanent harm to people or animals.

Federal law also punishes using the mail, telephone, telegraph, or an instrument of commerce to willfully make a threat or maliciously convey false information (knowing that it is false) about an attempt or alleged attempt to kill; injure; intimidate a person; or damage or destroy a building, vehicle, or property by fire or explosive.

Todd Fries' continuing actions against Mick and Karen Levine crossed city, county and eventually federal lines. Karen says, "So the FBI came in and Brian, I love Brian, he is the main thrust of this case. This would not have happened if not for Brian Nowak. And the reason he got involved was the bomb, the bombing." The chemical device, Karen's "bomb," in a very real sense blew up in Fries' face.

The Indictment

The charges against Todd Fries are as follows – pulled directly from the federal trial record summary.

A. Indictment

Count One of the second superseding indictment alleged that Fries:
did knowingly develop, produce, and otherwise acquire, transfer directly or indirectly, receive, stockpile, retain, own, possess, use, and threaten to use a chemical weapon, namely a combination of a chlorinated cyanuric acid and unknown reactive chemical component, which when combined,

created airborne toxic chemicals, including chlorine not intended for peaceful purposes, protective purposes, unrelated military purposes or law enforcement purposes as described in 18 U.S.C. 229F(7), by placing a device on the driveway in front of the garage and on the back porch or a residence... in violation of 18 U.S.C. 229(a) and 2.

Count Two alleged that Fries *"did knowingly and willfully make false, fraudulent, and fictitious material statements and representations, in a matter within the jurisdiction of the Federal Bureau of Investigation in violation of 18 U.S.C. 1001(a)(2). According to the indictment, Fries 'while impersonating another individual (initials M.F.) called the Federal Bureau of Investigation and falsely implicated a third person (initials U.C.N.) for the use of chemical weapons... knowing that J.C.N. had no connection to the offense... when, in fact, (Fries) was responsible for the use of the chemical weapons.*

The federal trial was focused only on the chemical device and the lying to federal officials. The numerous incidents occurring at Dove Mountain, such as animal cruelty, were largely ignored except for a few incidents which were used to establish an MO (modus operandi) for Fries' actions. Those other elements of the attacks would, however, be addressed in the state trial that was to follow.

Reliving the Nightmare

Mick was the first witness to testify, followed by Karen. The attorneys said they wanted them to testify first so that there could not be a claim later on that their testimony had been tainted by their exposure to other witnesses and the evidence presented. They were virtually in the dark as to what was happening and what had been planned for them. "We didn't know anything about the trial whatsoever. We didn't know who were to be witnesses. We didn't know what they knew and what they didn't know. All we knew was what we gave them, Mick says.

He adds, "The trial was a major thing for us. Some of the stuff we saw when they were burning the chemicals, because they showed movies in court, and we're looking at this device catching fire in seconds and it brings back all these bad memories."

Some of what had happened to them didn't really have its full emotional impact until the trial. Karen says, "It made us feel like –wow- we could have been killed. We had two doors open in Dove Mountain. He could have just walked in and killed us." That really hit home during those weeks.'"

The physical, mental and emotional strain of the trial was a burden. And the psychologists they were seeing at the time noted that both were suffering from Post-Traumatic Stress Syndrome.

Testifying brought back all the fear, confusion and torment of the nightmares they had endured. Mick says, "So, it kept happening over and over and over. It hasn't gone away."

Karen, too, struggled with reliving the nightmare. That struggle and the suffering it brought was the price of justice. "I was kinda' nervous. I'd never done that before. I did okay. It just brought back these bad memories. And with Mick being sick and then I had all this to deal with. Mick just had a transplant operation and then we had to go and talk. I don't know how I made it. Maybe some people just have that kind of will. God gives 'em that. I'm glad. This was really overwhelming."

Surprisingly, the nightmare extended into the trial. Mick especially was shocked at some of the witness statements. "There were other witnesses who were saying crazy stuff, too. We had never heard any of this stuff. We're hearing from the first time and we're going, "Holy cow, I can't believe this. Those incidents were real low points in the trial for me."

Karen says, "Up to the trial we didn't know anything about spoofcards, which is why we couldn't figure out how I had gotten the phone calls from the "bank" that weren't from the bank when this all started. Now, things were coming together for us and it was all being tied in."

Mick says, "He was calling into the FBI using these spoofcards which change your voice. And also puts a different phone number on the caller ID. That bothered me. I says, "Holy shit! What kind of mind would think up all this crap? It just fed more into what a whacko he really is."

One Crazy Story After Another

The craziness continued. Attorney Bock introduced one of Fries' Jewish friends as a character witness. The witness stated plainly that Todd Fries is not anti-Semitic. The witness said that Fries had been a guest in his home even on Jewish holidays.

The response from the other side can be summed up in the phrase, "so what?"

To this day Mick and Karen believe the attacks against them had nothing to do with anti-Semitism or any form of hate crime. As Mick says, "They told us right off the bat what Fries did wasn't a hate crime. So, why in a federal trial do you bring in somebody to say he is not anti-Semitic? It didn't make any sense. I think the lawyer was just trying to get it into the jurors' heads that the bombs couldn't hurt anybody."

Attorney Bock argued during his opening statements that the charges against his client were "trumped up." He stated, "The case at Dove Mountain and the case involving the Tucson Omni, ladies and gentlemen, is nothing more than a vandalism, a malicious mischief or a criminal damage."

Mick and Karen sat through three weeks of, in their words, one crazy witness after another. They're careful to note that the people weren't crazy – just their stories. For example, one of those crazy stories was also true - Fries' poop collection. The feces spread around the Dove Mountain and the Tucson National homes was human. Instead of scooping poop from a stable, a field or the grass along the sidewalks, Fries had his employees defecate into buckets, a fact some of them testified to in the trials. He stored this human waste for later use at the scene of the crimes.

A story in the federal trial is "crazy" when it's demonstrably false. Fries' alibi, for example. He claimed to have been riding his motorcycle with a friend the morning of the incident. When examined, the story just didn't hold up. For one thing, he trailered his motorcycle to his friend's house a long time before he was supposed to arrive. Supposedly he just sat around for that time period until his friend showed up, but that time frame was long enough for him to engage in carrying out his Levine 09 project.

Another defense strategy was to promote Todd Fries as a good businessman. Bock would say of his client, "He had a growing business, a business that was in excess, and I believe it would be around $300,000 a year. And the State of Arizona wants you to believe all of this is put at risk over a stop payment check."

And that strategy produced a number of curious business decisions. "He earned about $300,000 a year and spent $30,000 a month advertising. Twelve times $30,000 is $360,000 and he only took in $300,000. He is a great businessman. Doesn't make sense to me," Mick says.

Another defense move that made little sense was the claim that the chemical weapon wasn't really a weapon because no one was harmed as a result of the incident. The defense brought in a witness who stated that the chlorine gas produced didn't fit the definition of a toxic chemical. Bock would say the harm done by the chlorine gas cloud to the citizens of the community was at worst minor. "You are going to see that there was (sic) no injuries associated with this cloud, other than irritation, minor breathing problems, watery eyes, just like if you went to a pool that was over-chlorinated," he said.

The prosecution responded by reading the definition of chlorine which states that it is toxic. Struckmeyer in his opening remarks at the state trial noted the serous nature of the chlorine attack. "Now, these plumes of chlorine were not small by any means; right? Initially, first responders didn't know what they were. Hazmat was called. The bomb squad was called because the plume continued to grow. The estimate the officers (sic) at Northwest Fire Department that went said it was up to about a mile. It was dark, it was dense, and it certainly consumed that area of the neighborhood." He further noted that the first responders made attempts at evacuating the neighborhood. They even considered evacuating other neighborhoods nearby, but decided it was safer for the residents to remain inside their homes. The bomb squad was even called in and robots were employed to remove the devices Fries had planted.

Karen says, "When the feds brought in their chemist to testify we blew 'em out. Even the jury was laughing. That jury was a good jury."

The defense then says that no one took a reading of the gas cloud produced by the incident. Karen says that in her opinion Bock stuck with portraying the incident as little more than just a mischievous prank because he had no other course of action.

The prosecution, however proved the level of toxicity was well beyond lethal limits. The argument that the Levines weren't maimed, permanently injured or killed by the gas was like the gas cloud floating over Tucson National – it just blew away.

Something that puzzled and still puzzles Mick is the fact that the defense never really made an argument that Fries didn't commit the acts. "And you would have thought that they would have brought this up, that they would have pounded on it. This is all circumstantial evidence. Where's the proof he did it? They never brought that up at all. I thought that was strange," he says.

Another strange aspect of the trial, at least in the opinion of Mick and Karen, was Todd Fries seeming lack of concern about what was happening to him at the time.

Karen says, "We made eye contact. I just stared at him. He *smiled* at me. His grin, that grin was awful. I don't know why he was grinning all the time."

"He never gave up his smile, his stupid grin. He never stopped. When the jury came back and found him guilty, he still had this great big grin on his face. During the trial, I couldn't believe it. His life is on the line and he's laughing. He thought he was a movie star." Mick says.

Guilty Pleasures

The outcome of a trial, even when the evidence appears overwhelming, is always in doubt. Mick, Karen and the government's legal team, however, were as comfortable as possible with the probable outcome. Some were more comfortable than others. Mick says, "I'm listening to what's being presented to the jury and I'm scared about this. I don't know if I was scared purely because I was worried that they wouldn't find him guilty. I wasn't scared about what they presented. I was scared that one of those people in the jury would think maybe he didn't commit the crimes because they didn't prove it. It just takes one."

When the judge sent the jury to deliberate, everyone in the courtroom felt they would take a long time to reach a verdict. Mick needed to handle some banking business, so he checked with the attorney and advocate and was told, "This thing ain't coming back for a while. Do whatever you want."

Mick didn't even make it to the bank when his cell phone rang. The jury was back.

They had taken only ten minutes to make up their minds. A short deliberation generally means the evidence is so overpowering one way or the other that there is no real need for in-depth deliberation. Karen was confident of a guilty verdict. Mick was still worried.

When the foreman of the jury said "Guilty," Karen screamed, literally screamed in the courtroom. Her mother, who had been with them throughout the trial, screamed also.

Karen says, "I started tearing up. The jury looked at me and they smiled."

Mick could only think, "Thank God."

Judge Jorgenson sentenced Fries to 151 months in the Bureau of Prisons for unlawful possession and use of a chemical weapon and for providing false information to the FBI. A conviction for unlawful possession of unregistered devices carries a maximum penalty of 10 years in prison or not more than a $10,000 fine or both.

Karen was impressed by how Jorgenson handled the trial, especially the judge's muted sense of humor. "The federal judge was funny. Only because the one thing I'll never forget is when she was sentencing and she says and the biggest thing you did wrong was you had to pick on a defenseless elderly couple. I'll never forget that. This was when she was sentencing him. She was a really good judge. She was really for us," Karen says.

Fries reaction was puzzling. Mick says, "He was just sitting there like the Cheshire Cat again. Nothing. He had that big grin on his face and that was it."

To some in the courtroom it appeared that Fries didn't realize what had just happened to him. Karen says, "It was like he didn't realize... like he was on drugs."

Mick speculates that Fries has been a bully for all or most of his life. He got away with his actions because he pushed people around and they took it. Karen says, "Everybody was afraid of him. I don't think he believed he would be caught."

Mick says, "I'm not afraid of him today and I wasn't afraid of him then. As sick as I was, I wasn't afraid."

When someone is in the eye of the storm it can be difficult to realize just how big a situation he or she is facing. The case of Mick and Karen Levine was big news. It was covered extensively in local and regional media. The FBI even rated the conviction as one of its FBI Top Ten News Stories for the Week. The top case was the conviction of the infamous James "Whitey' Bulger, but case number two was "Phoenix: Former Tucson Businessman Convicted of Possessing 24 Explosive Devices."

Mick and Karen Levine weren't interested in being part of a big story. Then and now they would have preferred to have skipped this entire ugly, dangerous episode in their lives. They showed incredible will, stamina, patience and courage during the federal trial of Todd Fries. They would need those traits again because the next step was to enter the nightmare once again in a state trial. But before that could happen Mick and Karen would have to play a tortuous game of "hurry up and wait." Todd Fries appealed his case in federal court.

#

Post Script.

During the federal trial Sgt. James Paul of the Marana Police Department approached Mick and Karen and apologized for the department's lack of action. Karen says, "He came right up to me and said, 'I'm really sorry about this. We dropped the ball. We've known him for a long time. He's been in trouble for a long time, but we couldn't do any more about it.'"

*Bock declined comment due to the on-going nature of the case at the time this book was being written.

CHAPTER TEN

A TRIP TO LIMBO

Hamlet's "to be or not to be" soliloquy refers to "the laws' delay" as a burden born by those thrust into the arena. The legal system by design is a slow process and that's a good thing overall. But for a couple caught in a legal twilight zone the delay can be excruciating. As William Gladstone said, "Justice delayed, is justice denied."

One of the basic protections under the law is the right to petition for appeal, which, to no one's surprise, is exactly what Fries' attorney did. Would the long-sought victory be upheld or would an appeals judge find some reason to throw out the case? Although the prosecutors were confident of the sentence being upheld, Mick and Karen were forced back into the limbo of "hurry up and wait." And wait for ... what?

Karen says, "We won, but weren't really sure if it was going to go through the way we'd like it to go through because you never know about the appellate court. But I felt we were pretty safe."

The legal team felt that they had made a solid case, but that "what if" was always out there. Mick was concerned that somehow the team might have missed something and the appellate judges would cite some obscure point of law and reverse or minimalize the decision. "The appeal process is right. It's right to a point. We couldn't understand what that point of law could have possibly been. The attorneys didn't bring in extra witnesses. There was no hearsay. I mean, it was point blank – this is what happened."

Another factor, often expressed by Karen's mom, was the possibility of retribution from one or more of Fries' friends, associates or family members. Karen took it in stride as best as possible. She says, "I was pretty paranoid at times. Yes, I was, but I'm also pretty strong. I was always looking over my shoulder, but we didn't go out much. I only went out for maybe an hour or two, but I wasn't at a job where I'd have to worry for hours at a time out of the house. I basically stayed inside the whole time."

Mick wasn't as worried as his wife, yet he, too, faced that "what if" concern. He was out a good bit of the time and each of them had received considerable media attention throughout the years. "You just never know what's going to happen. I mean, if I'm out doing work somewhere and someone hears my name and they know who I am and what I went through…. I wouldn't know if it was a friend of his. You just don't know what you're going to get involved in. People know your face and your name," he says.

Finally Mick and Karen Levine got their day in federal court.

UNITED STATES COURT OF APPEALS
FOR THE NINTH CIRCUIT
UNITED STATES OF AMERICA
Plaintiff-Appellee

v.

TODD RUSSELL FRIES, AKA Todd Burns,
Defendant-Appellant

The case was filed March 30, 2015 before judges Richard C. Tallman and Johnnie B. Rawlinson, Circuit Judges, and Marvin J. Garbis, Senior District Judge. The opinion was written by Judge Rawlinson.

Fries challenged his conviction for using a chemical weapon in violation of 18 U.S.C. 229(a) and making false statements to the FBI in violation of 18.S.C. 1001. Fries contended that Congress exceeded its authority when it passed 18 U.S.C. 229 (a) to criminally enforce provisions of the Chemical Weapons convention. He also asserted that the district court erred in rejecting his proffered jury instruction on the jurisdictional requirements of 18 U.S.C. 229 (a).

Fries also claimed that the district court made an error in denying his motion to suppress evidence seized at his residence because the search warrant was "stale and overbroad." He also requested a new trial because, he said, the district court erred in admitting a co-conspirator's statements, and in rejecting his proffered instruction premised on the FBI's failure to record the phone call serving as the basis for the false statements charge. He also claimed that the district court erred in applying a two-level sentencing enhancement for obstruction of justice.

The Summary of United States v. Fries covers 37 pages and covers each of Fries' claims in detail. Specific cases precedents applicable to the case are cited. For the purposes of this book the Conclusion is the operative element of the Summary and is cited in its entirety.

IV. CONCLUSION

Taking our cue from the Supreme, Court's decision in *Bond*, we conclude that the prosecution of Fries pursuant to 18 U.S.C. 229 was within the federal government's prosecutorial authority. We also hold that Congress has the constitutional authority to proscribe the conduct in which Fries engaged. Unlike the defendant in *Bond*, Fries did not engage in purely local criminal activity resulting in minor injury to a single individual. Rather, his detonation of chlorine bombs requiring the evacuation of an entire neighborhood had "the potential to cause severe harm to many people." *Bond*, 134 S. St. at 2092 (citation omitted).

Interpreting the plain language of the statue, the district court properly rejected Fries 'requested jury instruction that 229 (c) required the government to prove that Fries' criminal act was against property owned, leased, or used by the United States. The requested instruction was legally untenable because 229 (c) states the jurisdictional elements in the disjunctive.

The district court properly denied Fries' motion to suppress evidence seized as the result of a search warrant. The information supporting probable cause to search was not state because it was based on Fries' continuing pattern of criminal conduct. The search warrant application sufficiently limited the agents' discretion in conducting their search of Fries' residence, computers, and business records.

Consistent with our precedent, the district court correctly held that the statements of Fries' co-partcipant were admissible pursuant to Fed. R. Evidl 801(d)(2)€ as co-conspirator statements even though the indictment did not allege a consspiracty count. The district court also acted within its discretion in rejecting Fries' proffered missing evidence instruction as lacking the requisite legal and factual support.

Finally, the district court did not err in applying a two-level obstruction of justice enhancement becaust Counts One and Two were properly grouped pursuant to U.S.s.G 3D1.2 and the enhancement was applied to Fries' conviction for use of chemical weapons. Fries' conviction for making false statement did not fully encompass Fries' obscructive conduct.

AFFIRMED

The court's response was summed up nicely back on page five of the Summary by Judge Rawlinson:

"We affirm Fries' convictions and sentence."

The decision was a victory, but the legal process was far from over. Mick and Karen celebrated, rested up, and then prepared for the next step.

CHAPTER ELEVEN

NOW IT'S OUR TURN

M ick and Karen dealt with mixed feelings about the federal trial. On one hand, the stressful situation was over and they had won. Todd Fries was a convicted felon sentenced to a long term behind bars. The constant "what if" fear of reprisals was over. They were free to begin rebuilding a life and to enjoy a lifestyle that didn't involve "looking over your shoulders" every time they left the house. On the other hand, they faced another trial at the state level, a trial that would be more complex and at least as emotionally draining as the first. The knowledge that it would all be over soon provided some relief.

"Soon" is a relative term.

Mick says, "After the federal trial ended we thought things would be okay because we were told that the state trial would begin right after the federal trial. But it wasn't all that okay. We were calling all the time trying to find out what was going and why wasn't the state pursuing this like we were told. We were calling Brian at the FBI and then Beverly on the federal prosecution team and then the state. We couldn't get through to anyone and then we were told that they couldn't do anything until Fries was through with his appeals."

The nightmare may have been over, but they were still trapped within a bad dream. How can someone begin a new life when the worst of the old life won't let go?

Two years later the Levines received a call from the state prosecutor handling the case, Malena Acosta. She invited them to her office so they could discuss the case, update them as to what was happening, and to prepare for the upcoming trial. The drive into downtown Tucson was no longer the nerve wracking experience that leaving the house had been. Fries was in jail and couldn't reach them. Karen's mother, however, continued to issue warnings that Fries had friends and associates who were "out there" and who could possibly continue the attacks. Mick did his best to reassure her that nothing would happen. He was confident, but, still, that annoying "what if" question hovered in the back of his mind.

They found Acosta more down to earth and easy going than the federal prosecutor. "I think Malena is more of a people person. Bev knew the law, but she just wanted to get through the case without ruffling any legal feathers. She didn't want to do or for us to do anything that might jeopardize the case," Karen says. Acosta would be assisted throughout the case by Assistant Prosecutor Sterling Struckmeyer. Mick and Karen learned that their case in terms of trials was considered a big case. Acosta later said, "For several weeks I had close to 50 witnesses where the issues were somewhat complex. It was a four year period in which Fries committed these offenses. There was the federal trial before, so there was this whole issue we had to research as far as double punishment issues in the sentencing. The trial was far from simple."

Mick's health had improved and as they prepared for the state trial; he wasn't as sick or as exhausted as he had been during the federal trial. His physical strength was considerably better which helped promote a more positive and upbeat attitude. "So it wasn't as hard on us – at first. It was sort of relieving at that point. Then it started to get a bit crazy again because we're reliving it all over again. Something we had forgotten that he had been sentenced in the federal trial – now it's coming back up again. And you have to think about it all over again," he says.

Karen was riding the same emotional rollercoaster. "We were trying to start our life over. We wanted to say it's all behind us now, but it wasn't. There was a lot of sadness going on and anger again because son of a gun here we go again. We have to sit through another trial and it's going to come out all over again. It was a kind of up and down thing. There were good days thinking he's not going to get out and there were bad days thinking we're going through this again. I didn't want to. I didn't want to have to go back there again. I just didn't want to live through it again. I was much better with health and I just didn't want to do it."

They were startled by something they saw at that first meeting. Acosta's office featured a large display of the case against Todd Fries His photograph was the center of a hub of photographs linking everyone involved in the case. The display looked like something out of a police procedural television show with photographs and images connected by multiple lines. Mick and Karen were impressed by the amount of investigation and work that chart represented. Mick says he would have felt considerably better and more confident during the previous two years if they had told him about how much effort the state was putting into the prosecution. "It was impressive. I just wish they had impressed me two years earlier," he says.

Mick and Karen made a positive impression on their attorney also. Of Mick, Acosta says, "I like him. They were under such stress, all of them, and Karen particularly. And Mick seemed to be a little more the anchor that held that couple together, the kind who would push through this. When Karen would start to lose it, he would be the more rational one. I was a little bit on eggshells when he was on the stand, though, because he has a bit of a temper. I knew he didn't like the defense. And we had talked about that – you have to be on your best behavior in front of the jury. You can't let the defense attorney get under your skin while you're up there testifying. I thought he'd do okay."

She sympathized with what Karen had been going through." So much anxiety in one little package. I felt horrible for her. You could tell that this hit her so badly and to be going through … since it first happened in 2008 and here we are taking him to trial for all his charges eight years later. And Fries was out for a year and a half before the feds charged him. That's a lot of time to build anxiety. She's the type who reacts first and thinks later. And like I said, I felt horrible for what they went through having to move so many times. She seemed to take it the hardest. Never feeling safe and always looking over your shoulder.

I'm hoping we get him held for a good long time so they can feel safe wherever they are," she said.

Those words brought an incredible sense of relief and hope. Karen says, "I felt good about it. Finally we hear, 'Now, it's our turn and we don't have the handcuffs on us they had in the federal trial. We're going after him for everything he did.' It was at that point a relief that just maybe we were going to get a bit more justice out of this trial." Justice is the key word. They weren't looking for revenge or payback. They just wanted the system, slow and ponderous as it is, to work as it is supposed to work.

When the indictments came down, Acosta sent them a copy and the state really did go after Fries on everything relating to the horror he had put the Levines through:

- Two counts of attempted first-degree murder
- Two counts of kidnapping
- One count of aggravated assault
- Three counts of endangerment
- Two counts of manufacturing, possessing, transporting, selling or transferring a prohibited weapon
- One count of arson of an occupied structure
- One count of burglary
- Four counts of taking the identity of another and
- Four counts of criminal damage.

Fries faced a 27-count state indictment, including two counts of attempted first-degree murder. He was also accused of arson, kidnapping, aggravated assault with a deadly weapon, endangerment and other crimes. He faced a14-juror panel, which included two alternates.

The indictments included a charge of kidnapping. That sounded like something of a stretch at first. But as Acosta explained it, according to the law Fries had committed a kidnapping. When he sealed the doors and windows of their home and left them only one way to get out, a way that was blocked with a potentially deadly explosive device meant that he had confined them against their will – the definition of kidnapping.

Swift justice is considered a right in the American justice system, but, as with the definition of "soon" previously mentioned, "swift" is also a relative term. The state trial against Todd Fries ran through three judges. And that process ate up a lot of time.

The first judge changed the original court dates because of a physical problem. She had to bow out of the trial. Finding a new judge whose schedule had a three-week slot took more than a year.

Another woman judge was selected. Mick's opinion of her was not good. "First of all I don't think she even knew the case because she didn't even know some of the basics. For example, she posted bond for him, a $75,000 cash bond. *Fries was serving a sentence in a federal prison* at that time. During the proceedings he was speaking on screen - televised from that prison. He addressed the judge almost like he couldn't believe what he was hearing. 'If I post $75,000 bond I'm free?' he said. The judge said yes. Malena reminded the judge that persons incarcerated within a federal penitentiary are not eligible for bond. Good grief."

"We couldn't believe it," Karen says.

The new judge set and cancelled dates for the trial. Mick was not pleased. "The judge says, 'I have to change the date because my son is graduating from the military academy and he's coming into town that week. So, I can't hear a case." Mick responded to her statement, "I don't give a shit." Mick is not known as someone who carefully hides his feelings. He says, the judge then replied with, "I understand that the victims are upset with that decision, but I don't care." She said that in court. I said to myself, I'm the victim here and I'm sitting in court and you're telling me you don't give a shit about me. That didn't sit real well with me."

The trial was postponed. The judge had made up her mind about the schedule and there was nothing the Levines or the state could do about it. Before the trial could begin their judge was assigned to another trial to cover a situation for another judge. The move created a conflict with the Fries case. The scheduled trial dates were no longer good, so the judge bowed out and the search for a third judge was on. It seemed at times that the game of "hurry up and wait" would never end.

Judge Richard Fields took on the case and heard it through the conclusion. Fields had been an attorney in private practice and had served 14 years as the City Attorney and Prosecutor of South Tucson before being appointed to the Arizona Superior Court for Pima County by Gov. Fife Symington in 1997. Fields is an avid outdoorsman and a skilled bowhunter. The walls of the courtroom were decorated with colorful prints of trophy animals, such as pronghorns, elk and turkey. The last print, by the public exit, featured a snowy mountain scene in which a cougar chases a turkey. The wood-paneled courtroom layout was basic and efficient. The back was reserved for observers who sat in wooden benches behind a low wooden barrier. Two tables were placed in front of this barrier – one for the prosecution on the left and one for the defense on the right. A jury box ran alongside the left wall. Sheriff's deputies assigned to the court sat in chairs on the right side of the courtroom. The court reporter's station was also located in the right side of the room. The elevated "corner office" was reserved for the judge whose bench was flanked by the American and the Arizona flags.

Mick and Karen were happy that the trial was at last going to happen, but they were also apprehensive about the outcome – a not guilty verdict was possible. They were also concerned about having to relive a physical, emotional and mental nightmare. And they would have to relive it in public and under examination by someone duty bound to attempt to discredit their story. Karen says, "We were trying to start our life over. We wanted to say it's all behind us now, but it wasn't. There was a lot of sadness going on and anger again because son of a gun here we go again. We have to sit through another trial and it's going to come out all over again."

They were back on the rollercoaster, experiencing good days and bad days – the inevitable ups and downs and mood swings. Mick was tired of the whole thing and just wanted to get through with the thing and move on. "I just didn't want to live through it again. I was much better with my health and I just didn't want to do it," he says. Karen says. "I didn't want to have to go back there again, either. We didn't want to see Fries again, but we weren't going to stop and let him get away with what he did. No way. This was our time."

Opening statements began March 15, 2016, the second day of the trial, with Malena Acosta and Sterling Struckmeyer on behalf of the State of Arizona and Richard C. Bock on behalf of the defendant. Struckmeyer opened for the state.

Bock argued that the events weren't as serious as the State claimed. In his opening statement to the jury he said, "So all we ask is you keep an open mind and consider the fact that this case is nothing more than vandalism." Once again he was attempting to define attacks that resulted in the evacuation of an entire neighborhood (and worse) as a prank that got out of hand. Mick and Karen knew that was a ridiculous argument, but the question remained: would a jury see it that way?

Bock never put Fries on the stand during the state trial. No one other than the attorney and client know the reasoning for that move, but Acosta posed a theory that might fit the situation. She said, "He's one of those people you look at and wonder who raised you? What was your mom like? What was your dad like? What made you do this? I just... like I said in closing arguments it seemed like these women confronted him and he couldn't take it. I don't know. He struck me as perhaps someone who had been bullied growing up and he turns around and bullies people, takes advantage of the fact that he controls his employees, and he couldn't control these women, these customers of his and it must have just burned him up inside. He is kind of a puffball, a bit of a wimp and I don't know. One of the reasons I wanted him put away for so long is that I feel like I'm the kind of person that he would want to retaliate against."

Perhaps Bock's rationale for keeping his client off the stand was that the less the jury saw of Fries the better his chances of acquittal.

Karen was first to testify and she expected a nightmare. Attorney Bock was again representing Fries and he had been tough on her during the federal trial. "Worse than his questions was just bringing up all the feelings from those incidents. It was just terrible," she says.

Fries was in court, but she tried not to look at him. Again, even a glance his way brought up even more unpleasant memories. Fries' seemingly cavalier attitude only made the matter worse. As in the federal trial he appeared unconcerned about the events circling around him. To this day neither Karen nor Mick know if Fries was legitimately unconcerned, disconnected from the truth, or just putting on a show. "If he was putting on a show, it was the damnedest performance I've ever seen," Mick says.

The jury was more low-key than the federal jury and they were harder to read. Karen notes that the federal jury was composed of older, more experienced people. She couldn't help wonder if the younger jury in the state trial might not see what Fries had done to them as a major crime. She wondered if they might buy into attorney Bock's argument.

In Mick's view, Bock was attempting an "everybody is lying except my client" defense. Acosta called it a "spaghetti defense." "You argue what you can and throw everything against the wall and see what sticks. That's all they had," she says. Fries was merely being mischievous and shouldn't be punished harshly for actions that just got out of control. Bock argued that Fries had not committed any of the crimes, claiming that the state was prosecuting the wrong man. He also argued that smoke from the devices was not toxic and therefore whoever set them off was not guilty of attempted murder.

Acosta's overall opinion of Bock was positive. "I think he did his job. He is always pleasant to work with. I've done other things with him and he's always very fair. I like it when attorneys can work things out ahead of time, make some agreements. For instance, I was annoyed that Bock kept objecting to all my photos and that the judge sustained the objections which is why my photos didn't come in. But for the most part, which is why I tried to show them to him ahead of time so we wouldn't have to argue the matter in front of the jury and waste their time and get on to the case. He was very for the most part, except for the objections to the photos, very easy to get along with for those things, and the interviews and all the pre-trial matters."

Mick felt that Judge Fields was often agreeing with too many of Bock's arguments. "And I didn't like that either. So I couldn't read this judge. He was supposed to be impartial." Karen adds, "Yeah, we didn't like this judge."

Acosta explained that in her opinion Fields was presiding in an extra cautious way to insure that the verdict, whatever it would end up being, would stand. He did not want to create or allow something that might create cause for an appeal. "I've been in front of him before. Sometimes I feel he is overly conservative – with the photos, for example." Judge Fields had not allowed all the evidentiary photographs wanted by the prosecution team. The number presented had to be culled. "In any other courtroom I think all of my photos would have come in, but he was trying his best to, number one, make sure that the trial was fair to the defendant, but, number two, that the case would be upheld on appeal, that there aren't any mistakes made so that when there's an appeal because, there will be, that the verdict holds rather than come back and everyone has to try it again. So that was even less evidence I felt in front of the jury, but overall I think he did well."

For example, to the surprise of everyone on the Levine team Judge Fields did not believe the attempted murder charge valid. Mick says,

"When they brought in the attempted murder, he said, 'I don't think that's going to fly, either. I wouldn't have let it in, but since that wasn't brought up before, it's in. The jury ain't going to buy it.' The jury wasn't in the courtroom at the time. I thought, 'Wait a minute, that's not for you to decide. He was indicted on that. It was brought to the jury on that. So, you're the judge and you're supposed to make sure everything goes down legally.'"

Acosta and Struckmeyer were concerned that the attempted murder charge might never be heard by the jury. Acosta says, "When it came to the attempted first degree and the judge was waffling on that, on Rule 20, I thought, "Gosh, that's not even going to go to the jury. I at least want a chance to take it to the jury. And the fact that the judge waffled gave me pause, but at the same time I thought yeah but this is why it should go to the jury. If the judge can't make up his mind it should go to the jury. And so, I was pretty pleased because judges see the worst of the worst day in and day out and they hear the worst things that people do to one another. But the jury, not necessarily so which is why it's great that it's composed of people from the community, lay people, most of whom – none in my trial - do not have a law background and they hear these things and that's their impression. You can tell by their questions that they're probably struggling with was he really trying to kill them. So the fact that they took their time in deliberations tells me that they just didn't rush just to get out of there, to be done with their service, that they took their time."

Mick and Karen were also concerned about an appeal or a mistrial, especially when some of the facts of the case weren't brought up in the order in which they happened. The chronology of events was something they considered a key element in the case. Fries' actions when presented as they occurred clearly showed an escalating pattern of violence. But they were told that the chronology wasn't all that important.

One of the things that hit Mick and Karen hardest was the feeling of being ignored in their own case. Mick says at the time he thought, "Nobody cares about *us*. They were all working to get a solid conviction, which is good. I was right with them on that, but somehow it seemed that Karen and I *as people* were sometimes left aside."

They were helped through the often confusing and generally frustrating justice system by a victim witness advocate as part of the Victim Witness Program Office of the Pima County Attorney. Francisco

J. Padilla proved to be a valuable resource. Pima County has one of the premier programs in the nation. Founded in 1975 it was the first in the nation to provide comprehensive assistance to victims of crimes. A staff of more than 25 persons is augmented by more than 120 volunteers. Padilla says, "A Victim Advocate isn't assigned to every case, but we were definitely called for in this one. Property cases, or fraud or theft cases, aren't as common for us as cases where someone is shot or injured. But if there is a victim who is particularly anxious and would like one of us on board, they can request one. Thinking about all they went through, I can see why Mick and Karen wanted an advocate."

Padilla lists a lineup of basic services the program offers. These include Inform victims of their rights, explain the criminal justice system and the roles of other parties, obtain victim input before decisions are made about the case, accompany victims to court and trial to provide emotional support, explain court proceedings, and answer questions, work with detectives and Deputy County Attorneys to address victims' or witnesses' concerns, inform victims of avenues for seeking financial restitution and property return, assist with writing victim impact statements, help with scheduling for court appearances, and make referrals to appropriate resources.

He says, "People coming to court, especially those who have never been involved in a serious trial, can find the process confusing, challenging and frustrating. Mostly, they think things move along like they do in television programs and movies. But this isn't *LA Law* or *Perry Mason*. It's the real thing and that can be a real struggle for some people."

He found Mick and Karen to be inquisitive about the process, expressing their concerns openly, but without being as pushy or nervous as some of his clients. "They were focused all the time, but they were always friendly with me. I try to be available by phone or e-mail if I can't be available in person. Some people abuse the privilege, but they never crossed that line – never even came close."

Karen says, "Francisco was nice. He tried to help us and explain what was going on. I think he did his job well – better than the advocate in the federal trial who was terrible. She was all about keeping us in line so they could do what they needed to do. They were more concerned about not upsetting the applecart than in being concerned about our feelings or needs."

Padilla says, "We do a lot for the victim. When the attorneys are busy it's easy to brush aside the victims and forget that their feelings need to be taken care of. All the victims usually see is the legal process. We know how to talk to them as people. We can listen to them, allow them to blow off some steam without becoming judgmental about the case. That's not our job."

Mick says, "Unless you've been in a really tough case, you can't understand what kind of rollercoaster a big trial like that can be. When we needed support, thankfully the county – Francisco – was there."

The state trial had its upbeat moments. Mick and Karen actually enjoyed hearing witnesses testify as to what had really happened. "Hey, our story was finally getting out there and it was supported by a lot of witnesses," Karen says.

Some of the witnesses, however, weren't enthusiastic about speaking in court or were not available. Kaylin Hovey did not request restitution and made no sentencing recommendation in the case. She did not invoke her victim's rights and did not attend the trail. Attempts to contact Joaquin Contreras Navarratte, and Linda Mott were unsuccessful. Michelle Fuentes and Jina Parks attended portions of the trial.

Marguerite Brown and her daughter were on the stand for one day only. She also sent a victim impact statement by electronic mail and requested to be advised of the disposition and of any further hearings.

Some of Fries' employees fit category less than cooperative participants. Mick says, "They absolutely did not want to be in there." He was told that the state had a real problem with one of the employees who said he would not testify, that he would not even show up. He wasn't going to testify. They told me this guy point blank told them, 'I'm not coming.' But they got him. The witness was one of the men who had helped Fries and he just didn't want anything to do with the matter again. He told the truth, but he didn't want to be there and everybody knew he didn't want to be there because of the way he was testifying." Karen says he had a "Can we get it done now so I can leave?" attitude. "In a way I think that helped us," she says.

David Trujillo, the supervisor for Burns Power Washing on the Levine's work, stated that Fries had asked him to help out with his "Levine Project." Fries had so many buckets of waste that he said he needed help getting the foul mess out of his truck and dumping the material on their driveway. Trujillo refused! He quit his job after learning that Fries had gone through with his plan of revenge.

The fear of a mistrial became very real. Judge Fields had not believed the trial would require five alternates, so only two were selected. Almost as soon as the trial had begun two of the jurors had to leave due to illness. A mistrial would be declared if there were not enough jurors to see out the trial to its conclusion. Karen says, "Oh, my Lord, a third trial. And that's what Malena says could happen. All I could think of was, oh, Lord, don't let that happen."

Acosta felt as confident as possible about the overall case, but was careful to maintain a full grasp of even the smaller matters. She says, "I've been working on this for years. I want to get him. I want to put him away forever. You know it's just those little things in doing a case this big that you don't forget. That your evidence is there. Every time I look at the case it can produce a bit of anxiety because of the number of witnesses and all the corralling that needed to be done – bringing in people from out of state and timing and everything like that. And then I remember, 'It's a good case. I had so much evidence against him."

The book you are reading now even became an issue in the case when Bock brought it up stating that their testimony would be tainted because of their participation in this project. That argument didn't fly. For one thing their testimony was already a matter of court record and couldn't be changed. Secondly, they had notified all parties concerned about the book project. Mick says, "We weren't hiding anything. We told them look we're working with an author to work on a book. We had had our say in court and now we wanted to have our say in public. We wanted to let everybody know about it." That issue was quickly dropped and the trial moved on to substantive issues.

Fries' motivation and his unusual and erratic behavior before and during the attacks and during the trail remained a mystery throughout. Why would an apparently steady and successful businessman go off the deep end over such trivial matters? Acosta says, "I'm not sure that there's a lesson here. Mr. Fries is not someone you could plan for. Obviously he ran a business and I think if anyone had checked his reviews they would have found good reviews probably. I don't think there's any way to know when something like this is going to happen. He had a bunch of cash in his safe and people working for him, a nice piece of property, and a business that was going great guns. Who knows? Some switch just flipped in his brain when he was challenged like this. Like I said, I don't think there is any way you can really anticipate or see this in someone necessarily."

An interesting feature of the trial allowed Mick and Karen to not only have their day in court, but also to have their say in court.

CHAPTER TWELVE

THE JURY FINDS....

M ick and Karen requested and were granted the opportunity to make a statement in court prior to sentencing.

Mick's Statement

"I would like to thank the court for this opportunity to express my feelings.

I would hope that Mr. Fries understands all of this but it does take a very, very sick mind to think it up and it didn't just take overnight but many, many years to perfect such horrific warped thoughts and deeds!

It has taken almost eight years to get to this point in time and many things have gone through our minds about it I have been told by all the experts that we will never really be over it. PTSD, which we have been diagnosed with will never leave us.

It took 24 people, your peers, members of two juries to see through all of this craziness you did. I feel sorry for all of them and sorry for the judge and court staff who had to look at your "Chesire Cat' grin throughout both trials. Your smugness only meant one thing, Todd, I guess you think you did win after all! I want you to remember that thought while in jail all of those lonely days and nights. All of it over nothing.

It's too bad there isn't a criminal charge for being "stupid out of season" because you certainly fit it to a "T"!

You not only attacked us once but had to come back and do it again because you weren't satisfied and you thought you got away with it like everything else bad you did in your life.

I personally think you thought we would have you clean up the mess you made to recoup the loss from the bad job you did in the first place. You must have thought I was that dumb!

At the second attack, which was of a much more serious nature with the bombs, trying to kill or permanently injure us you still weren't satisfied. You at that point took on an entire community without any thought of whom else you may injure.

Still you weren't done. You found another innocent victim in Marguerite Brown. Oh my, someone else whom had enough guts to tell you that you had done a terrible job at their home, so it starts again! You weren't smart enough to try different things to make it look different! Let's just make another mess of everything and maybe she'll hire me to clean it up… oops, she didn't either so let's get her also a second time. I'm almost glad that you did because everyone has had enough of you!

I really feel sorry for your mother and your family since they have had to live through your SICKNESS longer than we have!

Whatever time you are sentenced to will never be enough for us or for that matter, the entire Tucson community. If you ever get out of prison, with your twisted mind, you'd probably do it again to another innocent person.

On that note, in closing, I have a couple of more thoughts to express directly to you Judge Fields. Just two thoughts I ask:

1) What if you were my neighbor and had been home that evening/morning in 2009? What if you had been injured or even worse?
2) More importantly, what if you, Judge Fields, would have been the innocent victim on all or any of these occasions?

Karen's Statement

Your Honor,

I just wanted to say a few very important words.

These acts that Mr. Fries did to us were not just doing a few simple pranks like putting "firecrackers" around our house to scare us, but chemical devices, meant to explode and burn and seriously injure or kill us or unfortunately hurt someone else in our community. We were not the only victims!

These acts that Mr. Fries had done to us both in 2008 and 2009 caused our lives to be "a living hell."

His bad intentions were always very clear starting in the attack at our home in 2008 when he wrote "DIE JEW BITCH!"

Life as we have known it since 2008 has been one horrific roller coaster ride.

Mr. Fries made up his own rules feeling that no matter what he did it would be "no wrong."

He has felt no remorse in what he has done to us, then or ever.

Mr. Fries has always thought this to be a big joke, but it turns out to be a joke on him.

I am asking the court to give him the maximum sentence on every charge he has been convicted of so he can never do anything like this again to anyone else.

Todd Russelll Fries is one big menace to our Tucson community and society!

On March 31, 2016, day fourteen of the trial, the jury at last began its deliberations under the care of bailiff/law clerk Dani Dubois. "It was all over but the waiting, the wondering and the worrying," Mick says. He was the least confident of a guilty verdict. Karen was hopeful. Acosta, Struckmeyer and their team was as confident as possible, knowing that they had presented in their minds a solid case. The minds of the individual jury members were another matter. Acosta says, "Our biggest challenge was the possibility that the jury wouldn't see the case the way I did. We had his employees who were going to say the things they did that would put him there or whatever. We didn't have forensics on every scene the way I would like to see it."

Acosta and Struckmeyer were concerned about another aspect of the case. Todd Fries actions were so irrational that the jury might not believe such an apparently normal businessman could commit such a bizarre act. Acosta says, "And I was just afraid that they would be scratching their heads like "This doesn't make sense. Why would this guy do this?" And then consequently acquit him… that there was not enough proof that actually proved he was the one who did it. And so trying to get them to see that yes it is him and we don't have to have an explanation for why I think was running through my head the whole time I was running the trial. Irrational is the word. It wasn't like these women had done anything so horrible that he had to retaliate in this fashion. How would a jury react to the irrational?"

At 2:32 p.m. trial resumed with the defendant in custody attending. Agent Nowak was also present. Years of fear, intimidation, physical and emotional suffering came to a head at 2:36 as the foreman announced the jury had reached verdicts in the case. The court reporter read and entered those verdicts.

Attempted First Degree Murder, Count One – Guilty.

Attempted First Degree Murder, Count Two – Guilty.

Kidnapping, Count Three – Guilty.

Kidnapping, County Four – Guilty.

Aggravated Assault – Guilty.

Endangerment – Guilty.

Endangerment – Guilty. (The jury found that Fries also recklessly endangered Deputy Atwell with a substantial risk of physical injury, but not imminent death, proven beyond a reasonable doubt.)

Manufacturing, Possessing, Transporting, Selling or Transferring A Prohibited Weapon – Guilty.

Manufacturing, Possessing, Transporting, Selling or Transferring A Prohibited Weapon, Count Eleven – Guilty. (a second count)

Arson of an Occupied Structure – Guilty. (The jury found the defendant guilty of the lesser included offense of Reckless Burning.)

Burglary in the First Degree – Guilty.

Taking Identity of Another – Guilty.

Taking Identity of Another – Guilty (a second count)

Taking Identity of Another – Guilty (another count)

Taking Identity of another – Guilty (a fourth count of this offense)

Criminal Damage – Guilty (The jury found the value of the property to be $10,000 or more)

Criminal Damage – Guilty (The jury further found the value of the property to be $10,000 or more.)

Criminal Damage – Guilty. (The jury found the value to be $2,000 or more, but less than $10,000)

Criminal Damage – Guilty (The jury found the value of the property to e $1,000 or more, but less than $2,000.)

Attorney Bock asked that the clerk poll the jury. Each member affirmed his or her verdict. At that point a discussion was held between Judge Fields and counsel for each party. Fields then informed the jury that having found Todd Fries guilty of Aggravated Assault and Burglary in the First Degree it was necessary to determine whether the State had proven beyond a shadow of a reasonable doubt that those were the act of a dangerous man. He instructed the jury on the specific laws to be followed in deciding such an issue.

Assistant Prosecutor Sterling Sruckmeyer and Attorney Bock each argued their respective positions before the jury. The jury retired at 3:05 p.m. At 3:20 the foreperson announced that the jury had reached verdicts regarding the dangerous nature allegations. The clerk read and entered the verdicts:

"With regards to COUNT FIVE of the Indictment, the jury finds that the offense involved the use and/or threatening exhibition of a deadly weapon or dangerous instrument, to wit: improvised explosive device, PROVEN BEYOND A REASONABLE DOUBT. With regards to COUNT THIRTEEN of the Indictment (Count Twelve of the purposes of trial), the Jury finds that the offense involved the use and/or threatening exhibition of a deadly weapon or dangerous instrument, to wit: improvised explosive device, PROVEN BEYOND A REASONABLE DOUBT."

Mick notes, "When the jury came back with the guilty verdict Fields was shocked that they had no problem with it." Fields had earlier expressed the opinion that the jury wouldn't "buy" the charge.

Again, Bock requested a polling of the jury. Again, each member affirmed his or her verdict.

At 3:24 Judge Fields thanked the jury for its services and discharged them from further duty. Fields and the counsels conferred on a number of issues including sentencing date, a deadline for pleading, and other matters. The court then revoked Fries' release conditions and ordered that he be held in the Pima County Jail without bond until sentencing. A few other "housecleaning" matters were resolved and it was all over – almost.

Sentencing was set for June 13, 2016.

CHAPTER THIRTEEN

WILL IT EVER BE OVER?

The sentencing was scheduled for 10:30 a.m. Everyone on both sides was curious, apprehensive, nervous or just glad the thing was just about over. Within a short period of time, surely less than an hour, Mick and Karen could get about rebuilding or adjusting their lives. At last the nightmare was coming to an end.

And then there was a snag. Sentencing was postponed until 2:30 that afternoon.

Fries and his attorney wanted to present some testimonial letters to the court prior to sentencing, but apparently Bock's secretary had not put them in the attorney's documents for that day. He and his people were trying to locate copies of the letters. Fries' mother, who had attended many days of the trial, believed she had copies at her home in the Tucson area. Judge Fields ordered a break to accommodate the defense.

Karen notes that such delays were common throughout the process. At the time she said, "This stuff started even in the hearings in federal trial. Every time something came up where they wanted to set a time or date Bock would have an excuse. It didn't matter what it was; he had an excuse. Can't do this. Can't do it. Can't do it; I have a different hearing. I can't do this. I can't do that. This went on constantly all the way through federal and of course they had to go along with it. He postponed the trial – and, of course, we had to go to these hearings – three times. With stupid excuses. The judge finally got fed up and told him straight out in her courtroom, we were there, that there are no more changes.' I don't care what happens. We are going to trial on this day,' she said. And he's been doing it all through this trial. I don't think this is real. I think this delay is phony as hell."

Mick added, "It doesn't make any sense except that it pisses everyone off. That's what makes sense of it. This whole thing is a scam."

The delay was just one more hassle for Mick and Karen who throughout the process often felt like pawns in someone else's game. At the time, Mick said, "I understand what's going on. But the letters won't really make a difference, like my statement's not going to make any difference. The judge already knows what sentence he's going to hand down. So, okay we have a right and I understand the judge is doing it to see that it doesn't come back to bite him on appeal."

That was the legal and practical side of the case. Too often overlooked is the human side of any given case. At the time Mick said, "Nobody bothers to ask about us – what it's doing to us. Or are we available or about how time consuming it is for us. That's what they don't take into consideration, so again we are still the victims. The prosecution does what they want. The defense can do what they want. The judge can do what he wants and we have nothing to say about anything. But we'd better be in court to testify as to what he did so he can get convicted. The system isn't quite fair."

The unplanned delay was an extra emotional burden on Mick and Karen because June 13, 2016 was Shavuot, a Jewish holy day in which prayers are said for the departed. Certainly that fact was unknown to the court system, but that knowledge didn't take the sting or the hurt out of the moment. Mick said, "This is an important custom. Today's one of those days and we're supposed to be there. And I would be praying for my father just like Karen would be. But instead we weren't asked if we could make it today. We weren't asked if the thirteenth would be a bad day for us. We were just told this would be when sentencing would be held. They probably don't know. Jewish holidays aren't like Christian holidays like Christmas. But Jewish holidays aren't the same way because we don't follow the everyday calendar. We follow the Hebrew calendar. But nobody ever asked. It would have been nice for somebody to ask us."

Fries kept up his cavalier appearance and did not outwardly show any reaction at all. For example, when Fries returned to the courtroom just before the verdict was read he appeared to some observers to be enjoying his position. One observer said he looked as if he thought he was a celebrity walking the red carpet and waving to his fans.

Mick and Karen, having been through a similar experience during the federal trial, remained outwardly calm. Inside, they celebrated their long-time-coming victory over the terror that had plagued them for nearly a decade.

Judge Fields read through the charges and dealt out the punishment for each conviction – 24 in all – as court personnel and observers tried to keep count as the numbers rolled out. Some were "counting fingers" as Fields enumerated the years for each verdict. Within a moment they were re-using a number of fingers. Ultimately Fields was given a ten year sentence in state prison on top of the 17 years he had already received in the federal trial. His time in the state pen would not begin until completion of the federal sentence.

Mick and Karen liked the state's throw-everything-at-him approach. Karen says, "I figured he's going to be 65 when he gets out of federal and then the state sentence on top of that. Even if they don't find him guilty on one or two of the major things they're still going to find him guilty on some of the minor things. So he's got to get five, six, eight, ten years more. I thought hopefully he'll never get out. And that's what we wanted."

Acosta says, "I would have liked to have seen more time, believe it or not… that 27 years wasn't enough. But when someone has committed murder 25 to life is standard. So I guess this is fair. No one died. People were not seriously injured."

"That's true, but the attempt at 'payback' over a disputed $200 cost Todd Russell Fries 27 years behind bars. Wow!" Karen says.

Mick said, "It's the first time that he's shown any remorse and I don't think it was real anyway. He has never shown any remorse whatsoever. 'Oh, I'm sorry that this happened to the Levines. I'm sorry for what I did.' Nothing."

But at last the trial, the doubt, the confusion and the worry was over.

Karen says, "I said to myself, it just doesn't get any better than this."

CHAPTER FOURTEEN

AND NOW....

The trials are over. The guilty verdicts are in. The judge, jury, prosecuting and defense attorneys have moved on.

Mick and Karen Levine are rebuilding a life without having to look over their shoulders or in the rear view mirrors of their cars. A stranger walking through the neighborhood or a strange vehicle driving by is no longer a cause for concern.

Todd Russell Fries is behind bars, conceivably for the next quarter of a century. He once controlled is own life, his business, and he lives of his employees. The man who tried to control the lives of decent people who had done him no harm is now living a regimented life in which other people call the shots. His life, every waking and sleeping hour, is under the control of men in uniform – guards and prisoners.

The motive behind his madness remains a mystery. When asked if he believed Fries' actions were based on anti-Semitism Mick answers in the negative. "It came up that it was nothing to do with him being anti-Semitic. He was a bully all his life. People never stood up to him. He scared them. We didn't scare so easily and maybe that triggered what happened. Who knows?"

At the end of the state's trial Judge Fields had asked him why a seemingly rational and successful businessman who clearly knew how to conduct himself with the public could put himself in such a position.

Fries, in his timid voice, mumbled something of a "things just got out of hand" non-explanation-explanation.

Acosta perhaps made the best guess. She says, "I'm not sure that there's a lesson here. Mr. Fries is not someone you could plan for. Obviously he ran a business and I think if anyone had checked his reviews they would have found good reviews probably. I don't think there's any way to know when something like this will happen. He's one of those people you look at and wonder who raised you? What was your mom like? What was your dad like? What made you do this? As I said in closing arguments, it seemed like these women confronted him and he couldn't take it. He struck me as perhaps someone who had been bullied growing up and he turns around and bullies people, takes advantage of the fact that he controls his employees. But he couldn't control these women, these customers of his, and it must have just burned him up inside. He is kind of a puffball, a bit of a wimp. One of the reasons I wanted him put away for so long is that I feel like I'm the kind of person that he would want to retaliate against."

After nearly a decade of harassment, intimidation, fear and frustration it's fair to ask Mick and Karen Levine "Is it all over now?"

Mick says, "We lived in a gated community, with a guardhouse. Okay, you think you're safe. The second time, we lived in another gated community with a guardhouse. You think you're safe in there. Right now we live in a gated community – no guardhouse. But I think the only thing a gated community does is it stops people from drag racing up and down the streets. Anybody can get in. So, what's the gated community for? To keep us in? It doesn't keep people out. That knowledge stays with you."

Karen says, "I used to be a fun –loving person and now this has changed my whole personality. I'm short-tempered. Emotionally, I sometimes get panicky, like even when I see a contractor looking at me or somebody I don't know outside comes out of his truck or something. I don't know why I get that way, but because of what he did to me, I hate contractors. I think they're all not to be trusted. So, actually we don't hire a contractor anymore. We try to do everything ourselves even though it's hard, but we do it. When something like this happens to you and even though he's in jail you can't get it out of your mind and say, 'Okay, let's live our lives like we used to' because we're not. I know now that if somebody is out to get you, they'll get you. It doesn't matter. You're never safe. That's a hard thing to live with."

Mick adds, "We're relieved that he's in jail, but I don't ever think it will be over because of all the nightmare we lived through and it definitely affects how we lived then and how we're probably going to be living and how we're living now. Because there's always that thought in the back of your head, 'My God, anybody can do anything to you.' I don't really think it's over."

Karen says, "We went through hell, a hell many people wouldn't go through. But you can't let bullies rule your life."

Mick agrees. "Nobody hands you a good life on a silver platter. Nobody gives you your freedom or justice or anything really. If you're a real man, or a real woman, you stand up. You grab it with all your heart and you move on."

End

A DECADE OF TERROR – A DAY OF TRIUMPH

A contractor's promise of "a couple of days work" to repair a driveway became a nightmare of harassment, destruction of property, terror and attempted murder for Tucson residents Myles and Karen Levine. The dispute over a $200 payment led to multiple attacks on their homes and property and a total disruption of their personal lives – events that culminated in a pre-dawn, terror-filed flight to safety. Trapped within their own home – doors and windows sealed with industrial sealant – their only escape was blocked by canisters billowing a clouds of toxic chlorine gas so powerful that it required evacuation of an entire neighborhood.

The Levine Project documents their struggle against a man focused on a personal vendetta; the physical, mental and emotional costs of standing against a determined attacker; and their decade-long battle for justice in state and federal court.

CPSIA information can be obtained
at www.ICGtesting.com
Printed in the USA
BVOW06*0237060917
494093BV00005B/17/P

9 781490 783772